FIDDLEBACK

MW00873472

FIDDLEBACK

BY ELIZABETH HONEY

ALFRED A. KNOPF

NEW YORK

HONEY

THIS IS A BORZOI BOOK PUBLISHED BY ALFRED A. KNOPF
Text and illustrations Copyright © 2001 by Elizabeth Honey.
Jacket illustration © 2001 by Mike Reed
All rights reserved under International and Pan-American Copyright
Conventions. Published in the United States of America by Alfred A. Knopf, a
division of Random House, Inc., and simultaneously in Canada by Random House
of Canada Limited, Toronto. Distributed by Random House, Inc., New York.
Originally published in Australia by Allen & Unwin, 1998.
KNOPF, BORZOI BOOKS, and the colophon are registered trademarks of Random
House, Inc.
www.randomhouse.com/kids
Library of Congress Cataloging-in-Publication Data
Honey, Elizabeth.
Fiddleback / by Elizabeth Honey.—1st ed.
p.   cm.
Summary: Twelve-year-old Henni records her account of a camping trip with
friends and neighbors.
ISBN 0-375-80579-6 (trade) — ISBN 0-375-90579-0 (lib. bdg.)
[1. Camping—Fiction. 2. Family life—Australia- Fiction. 3. Australia—Fiction. 4.
Diaries—Fiction.] I. Title.
PZ7.H7465 Fi 2001
[Fic]—dc21   2001029324

Printed in the United States of America
10 9 8 7 6 5 4 3 2 1
First American Edition: June 2001

For Juanita

With thanks to Ian Edwards, Ulrich Graf,

Tim Carrigan, Paul Connor,

and Rare Woods, Melbourne.

Front cover

Mum and Sue said, "people knit for babies," so when we saw wool and knitting needles at the op shop, we bought them. This weird-looking clomp of ~~knitting~~ Knotting! grew bigger than a bootie, bigger than a hat, bigger than a baby's sweater... It wasn't the right shape for anything except, maybe, the cover for a hunchback hot-water bottle.

gumnut
gumnut
gumnut
gumnut →

Heart of the Pool our best treasure

fiddle back

by Henni Octon

Zev's expert magnifying-glass leaf burning He said, "Make the name something that fits on two leaves."

Dried head of a poor little Dusky Marsupial Mouse. (Adios Antechinus swainsonii) from Heap. Third best treasure.

gummy bears

Feather from a now not-so-cocky cockatoo!

Contents

1 *Churr!*   1

2 My Sister, Danielle   2

3 Who, What, When, Where?   6

4 Cramping!   15

5 Christmas   21

6 Blast Off!   24

7 Through the Gate   28

8 A Wild Place   32

9 We're Never Leaving   37

10 Skinny-dipping, or Free Willies II   45

11 Cool Pool Days   49

12 A Miss Dippy Flip-Top Disappears   53

13 Possums? Fairies?   56

14 Catching the Possum   59

15 A Lot of Swearing   70

16 Place of Spirits   73

17 Platypus 79

18 Looking for Old Jim 84

19 Five Kids and a Hermit 90

20 Old Jim's Hut 94

21 The Dulugar 100

22 Mad as Meat Axes 109

23 Bombast 119

24 A Visit from Joe Blakes 127

25 The Tempest 133

26 After the Storm 140

27 The Stella Street Tribe 144

28 A Hitch 160

29 Zev's Idea 163

30 The Day Between 174

31 A Splash in the Water 178

32 "Have You Got Five Minutes?" 192

33 Heading Home 197

34 How Was Your Vacation? 199

FIDDLEBACK

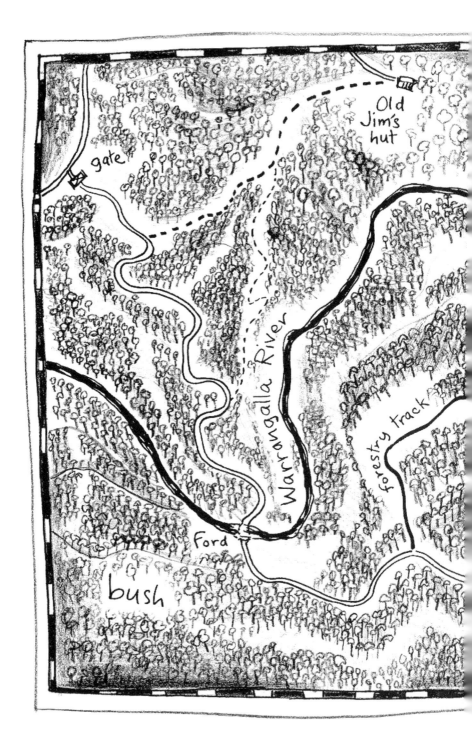

Fiddleback Map

bush

a long way

N

Fiddleback tree

The Gully

Little Creek

big ridge

Ruin

Reading Room

Bacon Flat

The Pool

Talk Rocks

1
Churr!

← Tibor's computer starting up! Love that sound.

I can't believe I am actually sitting down to write a book!

I MUST *be* Mad!

My first book was a total sellout—all eleven copies gone! (Actually, I gave them away.) But what a story I have to tell! Bits of it may be shocking to some people. I bet they'll say, That sort of thing is better left unsaid. But we all live our lives in different ways, and this is the way we live ours. Good writing is true, and this will be as true as I can make it—the way I see it. Anyway, nobody is making you read this story.

I'll call it *Fiddleback*. Strange word, bumpy like a knuckle. We didn't know what it meant, but we sure found out.

I'll write it for Donna and Little Jim and the fiddleback.

1

2
My Sister, Danielle

Before I tell you what happened, I will introduce myself. I'm Henni. I'm tall, I want to be a writer, and I'm going to junior high school in two days' time. At my old school, there were twenty-five kids in sixth grade. At junior high school, there will be about a *hundred and eighty* in seventh grade! Then I was a big (tall) fish in a small pond. Now I'll be a small (tall) fish in a big pond. (Zev calls me the Human Bookmark.)

This year I'm the proud flasher of a fabulous travel pass. With it I can go anywhere in zone 1 on trams, buses, or trains! It's very expensive and has my photo on it, and I bet I lose it. My little laminated magic carpet. I told Frank it was my driver's license, and he believed me!

We're getting organized for school, buying all the new things I need. I think this time of order is extra cool because it's such a contrast to our wild vacation, which wasn't meant to be so primitive, it just happened that way. Circumstances beyond our control.

The crowning glory of my new uniform—my blazer! With shoulders! It looks so grown-up.

My blazer has a lining. My first lining. My arms slip down

the cool sleeves. And in the lining over my heart is a secret inside pocket. If I ever get a letter from my beloved (if I ever get a beloved), that's where I'll put it, close to my heart.

You could sit a couple of Donna's pot plants on my shoulders!

"Don't you love it? It's silk," I told Mum.

"It is *not* silk," said Danielle. "It's something made out of petroleum."

Danielle is watching all this fuss about me. Of course, she has new things for school, too, but they're not totally new and different like mine.

When Dad came home from work, I got all dressed up in my new uniform, did my hair, and made the big entrance.

"Well, look at *you*," said Dad, putting his arm around Mum. "Clothes maketh the woman."

"And *breasts*!" said Danielle.

For nine long embarrassing years, Danielle has been my sister. Her motto is "Go forth and embarrass Henni," but now she is reaching more embarrassing heights than EVER!!!!!

"Danielle, don't be so rude!" said Mum in a resigned voice. "Go and slip on your new Windcheater to show Dad."

"You're just trying to make me feel better because Henni's getting everything. I know, 'when I get my blazer, it'll be special,' but it won't be so special because Henni wore it first and everything happens to Henni first. So what! Who cares! I don't!" And she stomped out.

A bit later, I went out into the backyard and Danielle was lying in the hammock breaking a stick into little bits and flicking them at a tea towel on the clothesline.

"Don't be such a pain," I said. "*You're* the lucky one!"

"Oh yeah?"

"*YES!*" I said, then I let her have it. I'd been storing up the ammunition.

"*I* had to sit at the table till I'd eaten *everything* and wait until everybody else had finished before *I* could leave the table. *I* had to be in bed at exactly eight-thirty. *I* didn't get pocket money until I was *seven. You* get more pocket money than I *ever* got."

"So?" She flicked a stick.

"*Hoh! You're* having an *easy* time. Mum and Dad don't fuss about *you* the way they fussed about *me*. Go and look at those bringing-up-children books on top of the fridge. All that underlining was done for *me*."

"I wouldn't mind being underlined," said Danielle.

"You're *kidding*! You're spoiled. You get away with murder."

"I never murdered anyone."

"No, but *I* might murder *you*, you excruciating little prune."

Silence.

"Yeah, I know," she said. "Sorry, Hen."

A bit more silence. I was just feeling human toward her and about to give her a hug or something when she chipped in, "Besides, you're older, you'll die first!"

I tipped her out of the hammock.

3
Who, What, When, Where?

It was a week before Christmas, at Zev's place. We all agreed we wanted to have a vacation together before school started again at the end of January. We all live on Stella Street. I'm going to do this like a theater program because I can't be bothered writing about everyone. Here's we:

Mum   Danielle   Me   Dad

The Octon Family

I'm going to say something about Mum, because it might seem like she's invisible. (I guess that's why they have Mother's Day.) It's strange talking about your mother. Her name is Claire, and I'm like her—a thinker. (Well, I like to think I'm a thinker.) Mum says, "It's not what you say, it's what you do."

Frank

Briquette →

Rob

Donna

The O'Sullivans who live at 47 St St.

Donna, as you can see, was *very* pregnant. She had just left her job, where she tried to patch together a life for kids whose families were falling apart. Donna had a hard time leaving work because the plans she'd made for this hopeless kid called Heap came totally unraveled, and she was stressed out. Everyone was glad when she finally came home with her enormous goodbye bunch of flowers and a huge book on Australian plants.

Donna's baby was everybody's baby. We felt the bump, and talked to the bump, and watched it grow bigger. First we called it Baby Dim Sum, then Baby Lemon, then Baby Orange, then Baby Mango, then Baby Cantaloupe, then Baby Football, then Baby Watermelon.

7

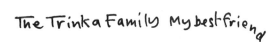

The Trinka Family My best friend →

Tibor   Sue   Zev

Zev's my best friend, and this year we're going to different schools. We toddled off to kindergarten together all those years ago, then we tottered off to elementary school together a year later. There's a photo of us on our first day: cute little Zev, with his spiky blond hair standing straight up on end, wearing his little Martian T-shirt, and cute little Henni in her cute little blue shorts with tropical fish, and a bow in her hair that's bigger than her head. We're holding hands, and if you look carefully at our faces, you can see we've been smiling for a long time.

When we got to school, we found they'd split us up. I cried and cried and cried. Zev was cool. He was funny about it. Well, our friendship survived then. I guess it will this time, too.

Zev won a scholarship to the Galileo School, where they're hot on science and technology. He's going to love it. They're going to love him! He's got a special interest in electricity. You see, there's something weird about his body—if he combs his hair really fast, sparks fly out! (Which can be very handy at times!) One day he's going to win a Nobel Prize for some electrifying discovery, you'll see.

May   Cass   Maggs

The Lees who live at 45 St St.

These are new friends who moved in next door to Frank.

They're arty. Maggs makes pots. They always wear bright, bright colors, and they eat funny food. (If you're ever offered squid in its own ink, don't do it! It's revolting!) Their house, 45 Stella Street, is chaos. When Maggs wants it to look neat, she drapes sarongs over everything.

Cass is in fifth grade this year. Her real name's Cassandra. She's somersault-mad, which spread to Danielle, so now they're both somersault-mad. (Tibor calls them the Misses Dippy Flip-Tops.) Cass has wavy hair and freckles. She's creative. Not very good at schoolwork. Can't spell for peanuts. But she comes out with great words that I wish I'd thought of:

"Cass, why didn't you finish your project?"

"I was feeling *unwritative*."

May's in fourth grade. She has short hair and is quiet.

Like me, she's a reader, so I'm passing on all my fourth-grade favorites to her. She has goldfish and a mouse called Cheezy.

Mr. Valentine Nicnac. He was born on St. Valentine's Day. The adults call him Val.

That saved a lot of explaining! (Or did it?)

So we all agreed to do something together during the Christmas holidays. Us kids listened with our ears pricked. Briquette was lying asleep on the floor, and every now and then her stomach grumbled as it tried to digest some disgusting thing she'd eaten. Briquette's a guts, and the more disgusting the stuff is, the more she loves it.

Mr Nic
who lives up
the street

How can I digest
this ?

"Vacations have to be a change of texture," said Dad. "You need to get out there amongst it."

"What do you suggest we get out there amongst?" said Mum.

"What would *you* like to do, Donna?" asked Dad. "You're the special one. You can have anything you like."

"Anything?"

"Within reason."

"Okay," said Donna, with a little smile. "I want to go camping." She turned to Rob. "I want you to get rid of that saggy old red waffle Lilo with the slow leak, and buy a comfortable new air mattress."

"Mmmmm?" said Rob slowly, not too enthusiastic. "And *where* are we going camping?"

"Picture this," said Donna, relaxing back in her chair and spreading out her arms to the imaginary blue sky. "A river flowing over smooth stones warmed by the sun. A pool where we can have a dip. Old gum trees, and nobody around but us. That's what I want."

"Sounds fabulous," said Rob. "I'll ring up and make a reservation."

"Wouldn't you like to be by the sea?" said Sue, straightening her blouse. "I know a great house we could borrow."

"No," said Donna. "I want to go bush. I want a glorious peaceful spot to remember when I'm getting up in the middle of the night to feed my screaming baby. When I haven't had a good sleep for months, I want to think of lying on a lounge chair, drifting and dreaming with never a care."

"Our baby's not going to cry," said Rob. "It's going to be perfect."

"Wouldn't you be more comfortable in a cabin somewhere in a national park?" said Tibor.

"Bit late for that," said Mum. "Everything will be booked by now."

"How will you go to the toilet?" asked Danielle.

Donna laughed. "Rob'll figure out something."

Rob still didn't like the idea.

"What if the baby comes early?" said Sue. "You're pretty close to your time."

"I've never been early in my life," said Donna.

"You're right there!" said Rob. "Frank was ages overdue. We thought they'd have to smoke him out!"

Frank pulled a choking face.

"I feel fine," said Donna. "We'll take it easy. It won't be a problem."

"*You've* never been early, but the baby might be an early person," said Sue.

Donna wriggled herself more comfortable, clasping her hands on the bump like a satisfied church mouse.

"Sue, you've got time off. Tibor can get away. Rob's okay. It's cheap. It's what I want. Let's do it straight after Christmas."

"Set off Boxing Day," said Dad.

"*Nooo!*" wailed Cass 'n' May.

Maggs pulled a long face. "We can't make it then. May's been invited to Sydney with a friend, and I *promised* Mum I'd sort through boxes of stuff with her. I've put her off twice already. Cass *was* going to her father's. . . ."

"Change it! Change it!" we chorused.

"Oh dear," said Maggs. "I don't like my chances."

"We'll take Cass," said Mum. "No problem."

Cass grinned and gave her mother a happy little wave. May looked extremely downcast (which was funny because Cass had been complaining that she wasn't going to Sydney).

Then everyone looked at everyone else with an optimistic what-do-you-think expression on their face. It sounded great!

"Well, that's the who, the what, and the when," said Dad. "What about the where?"

"I'll ask my sister, Miriam," said Donna. "If such a place exists, she'll find it."

"If we all scout around, we should come up with something," said Dad. "Another meeting in a couple of days?" Dad can't stop himself. He has to organize.

"Pizzas at our place, Thursday night," said Donna. It was a good sign. Donna was her bold old self again.

Danielle and Cass were already out in the hall doing

cartwheels of delight, with Briquette barking along deliriously.

"Camping, Briquette! Camping!"

"What did Old Auntie Lillie* use to call it?" asked Frank.

"Cramping!" we all said at once.

When we got home, another good reason for going cramping became clear. Danielle had the new single by the Noizeeboyz, "Rock-o-matic." She danced to it and played it sixteen times in a row. Dad got so fed up he went outside and turned the power off. Then we had to reset all the clocks. It was worth going cramping to get away from the Noizeeboyz. We were seriously sick of that song.

* Sweet Old Auntie Lillie lived in Cass'n'May's place before she died.

4
Cramping!

Donna's sister, Miriam, took up the quest for a good camping spot. She asked Old Jim. Now, Old Jim was a friend who'd been employed by the state government to kill dogs in the High Country not far from Miriam's farm. ("Dogs means dingoes," said Rob, "mostly crossed with German shepherds or something by now.") Old Jim had lived on his own in the hills for most of his life. He didn't have much time for people, but Miriam and Donna were okay because Jim had liked their mum. "I'll tell you the story sometime," said Donna.

Anyway, Old Jim had taken a stick and drawn a map of this place in the dust. Miriam remembered it, drew it on paper, and faxed it to us.

"If Miriam says Old Jim says it's a good spot, it's a good spot," said Rob.

Dad was a bit doubtful about the vague map. "What if she's forgotten some little turnoff. We could be totally bushed."

"Well, nobody's come up with anything else," said Sue.

"Old Jim's spot it is then," said Dad.

After that, there was talk about four-wheel drives and if it

would be all right to take an ordinary car. Donna rang Miriam to check.

Then there was talk about inviting Mr. Nic. Did we really want to? His cheerfulness can be a bit annoying. Then Frank piped up, "Mr. Nic's coming!"

"How do you know?"

"I asked him."

That settled that! You can't uninvite Mr. Nic.

Then Danielle said she wanted to bring Sarah from school. But Sarah is like an audience for Danielle and thinks everything Danielle does is ecstatically funny, so if she came, Danielle would show off nonstop, and it would break up the Stella Street family. We had all just taken a breath to say why Sarah shouldn't come, when Danielle said, "No, I don't want Sarah."

Maggs said we could borrow her huge army tent. It had been lost for years, but she refound it when they moved into Stella Street. There was a tear in one side, and it might not be waterproof, and it was very dusty. "Apart from that, it's great," said Maggs. "Easily big enough to take all the kids."

"Yesss!"

The day after school ended, Dad dropped us kids, and the tent in all its bags, and Maggs's how-to-put-the-tent-up diagram, round at this park near our place because we needed the space.

"Come and get me when you've got it up," said Dad.

For the first ten minutes, Danielle and Cass did handstands and cartwheels, frontsaults and backsaults, summersaults and wintersaults, insaults and outsaults, and every other possible sort of sault. (They're always leapfrogging over each other, or carting each other around, or standing on their heads.)

I was a bit embarrassed about putting up our tent in the park.

"We'll tell 'em we're rich street kids," said Zev.

"No. We're a circus!" said Danielle. That was the truth!

So, after ages, with me and Zev doing all the thinking and yelling and looking at Maggs's diagram, we got the tent up (with a bit of help from a couple walking their Irish setter, and a jogger who used to be a scout). It was big all right. And strong. And ripped. And heavy! And so *cool!*

We zipped ourselves in, and Danielle and Cass did cartwheels around inside. The gloomy green was like being underwater. Briquette barked like crazy outside, and tried to jump through the tear, and tore it even more. We zipped ourselves out, and Danielle and Cass did cartwheels around the outside.

"Danielle," said Cass, "go and tell your dad the tent is up."

"Frank," said Danielle, "go and tell my dad the tent is up."

"Briquette," said Frank, "go home and tell her dad the tent is up."

"Briquette, fetch Dad!"

"*Aff aff aff*," said Briquette.

Zev finally went back, because he had to make a phone call.

Then Dad arrived with special tent-waterproofing paint. We must have looked pretty funny, painting a tent. It was rather streaky. We spread old sheets everywhere so we wouldn't get any paint on the park.

Then Rob borrowed a heavy-duty sewing machine. (Rob is a junk dealer and knows where to get anything.) He set the machine up in the backyard, and Donna and us kids sewed a patch over the rip.

Now, that was a big job! We held out the skirts of the tent, like bridesmaids managing an enormous streaky green wedding gown. Donna muttered instructions as she gently fed the canvas under the foot of the sewing machine. Slowly, steadily she eased it through so it had no wrinkles and the patch was straight. (It made me think of how she eases people along and sews them together as families, with straight strong seams that she hopes will stand life's wear and tear.)

It was great having Donna around all the time.

Then we waterproofed the bits of tent we'd missed and the patch.

"The tent's finished!" sang Cass, giving a little skip before she hurled herself into a handstand.

"All this trouble is a guarantee it won't rain!" said Donna. "It's always the way."

On Friday evening, our family went prowling around the bushwalking shops in the city. I love outdoor shops. Boots, and clippy gadgets, and tents, and packs with pockets and buckles, and clothes for keeping you warm if it's freezing and cool if it's boiling, and contraptions for cooking on ice floes, and sleeping on cliff faces.

After having a good fiddle with everything, and pestering the parents to buy all sorts of great camping stuff, we each picked a bright plastic bowl.

"We should at *least* get mugs to match," grumbled Danielle.

"Come on, the parking meter's going to run out," said Mum.

5
Christmas

To tell the truth, Christmas was disappointing. The presents were good, but the actual day didn't feel like the Main Event.

Guess what Zev got from Rob and Donna? A nifty flashlight

```
**    **    I     **    **    **    **    **    **    **    **
**    **Danielle**    **    **  **    **    **    **    **
**    **  Cass  **    **    **  **    **    **    **    **
**    **  May  **    **    **  **    **    **    **    **
**    ** Frank **    **    **  **    **    **    **    **
```

From Sue and Tibor, Danielle got a funny duck pen

```
**    **    **    **    Frank  **  **    **    pig    **
**    **    **    **    May    **  **    **    bird   **
**    **    **    **    Cass   **  **    **   mouse   **
**    **    **    **    I      **  **    **    frog   **
**    **    **    **    Zev    **  **    ** tuning fork
```

From Mr. Nic, Zev got a packet of Minties

```
**    **    **    May   **  **    **    jelly beans
**    **    **    I     **  **    **    Jaffas
**    **    ** Frank   **  **    ** Gummy Bears
**    **    **Danielle**  **    **   Smarties
**    **    ** Cass   **  **    **Violet Crumbles
```

We gave Cass a red mug
**   ** Frank ** yellow **
**   ** Zev ** purple **
**   ** Danielle** blue **
**   ** May ** orange **
   I got ** green **

From Maggs, Danielle got a tennis ball
**   ** Frank ** ** ** **
**   ** Zev ** ** ** **
**   ** May ** ** ** **
**   ** Cass ** ** ** **
**   ** I ** ** ** **

Each family got an "IOU a plant" from Donna.

I won't go through all the presents, but I will tell you about Zev's because the presents he gave were so cool.

Zev set up a little business a few months ago, and he's earning heaps. He calls himself Captain Techno. All these people who don't know how to work their videos, or reset the clock on the microwave after the power's gone off, or get their computer to do things, well, Zev goes around and fixes it, or shows them what to do. He's really good. He started off putting little advertising notes in the mailboxes around Stella Street, but now Captain Techno's getting phone calls from everywhere.

He gave me a new thesaurus and a rhyming dictionary. I gave him three new combs. (Zev has a fantastic collection of combs for his amazing hair.) Danielle and I "combed" the market for them. It's really hard to come up with a new one now, he's got so many.

We wanted to get Zev a gadget, too, but the only thing we could find was a pen with a little light in it. We didn't think it was much, but he seemed really pleased.

But the best Christmas present was the walkie-talkie Sue and Tibor gave Zev. Perfect for camping. It was the first thing Zev packed. Even before his inventions bag.

That's why Christmas seemed flat: we were going camping! I felt really sorry for May, missing out.

6
Blast Off!

"How many days to next Christmas?"

"Three hundred and sixty-four."

"How many days to cramping?"

"*NONE!*"

Danielle was so hyper we had to sit on her.

Before anyone was up, Mr. Nic arrived full of beans at Rob and Donna's with his kit bag and an ancient canvas cot that was patched a thousand times. Rob looked at it, horrified.

"I helped to win the war sleeping on that cot," said Mr. Nic proudly.

Rob grabbed his cell phone. "Maggs, can Val borrow a comfortable, light, modern, twenty-first-century cot from you? Good."

"You've just been upgraded to first class," he said to Mr. Nic.

We were the runners, zapping messages from one house to another.

"Can you go and check if Tibor's put in extra cylinders for the lanterns?"

"Did Rob say he had jumper cables?"

"Tell Sue not to worry about tomato sauce. I've got three huge bottles."

The phone would ring. "Hang on two jiffs, I'll just grab 'er."

"Yes, we'll bring our big barbecue tongs."

"Give Donna a hand."

"Could you check what Frank's put in?"

"I finished packing!" yelled Frank, proudly zipping up his bulging bag.

"You're still in your pajamas!" said Zev.

Then something started buzzing from the bottom of Frank's bag. The Alien Blaster game on his key ring.

"You have to have 'game over' before you turn it off," said Cass.

It was like that.

Of course, our tent, which became known as the Big Top, was the largest item to be packed.

"And this," said Maggs, dumping a folded-up carpet on Rob's foot, "goes with the tent. We always used it. Pop it in. You've got room."

Rob and Donna were well organized. Donna had a special box for all her botanicalizing stuff. She's a fantastic gardener. Loves plants.

Between us all, we had boxes and boxes and boxes of food, including Donna's famous industrial-strength banana cake (which wouldn't last long), and her Adults Only fruitcake with grog in it (which wouldn't last long), all the scrummy Christmas leftovers, enough pancake mix to feed China, and an hour's worth of 2 Minute Noodles.

"We'll never eat all that!" said Dad.

"Want a bet?" said Sue.

Tibor put in a bag containing every conceivable type of string, twine, and rope.

"I've got the kitchen sink in here!"

"No, Tibor," I corrected him. "You say 'everything *but* the kitchen sink' in here!"

He gave me his funny twisted smile, where his eyebrows go up and down at the same time. (Tibor came to Australia when he was twenty, and although his English is perfect, he occasionally gets his sayings slightly wrong.)

Everyone packed their Christmas books. Donna put in *What Plant Is That?*; Tibor put in *What Knot Is That?*; Sue put in *What Bird Is That?*; Mr. Nic put in *What Wound Is That?*; Rob put in *What Baby Is That?*; Dad put in *What Star Is That?*; and Danielle said she put in *What Cute Little Marsupial Biting a Hole in Your Lilo Is That?*

Everyone wanted to travel in someone else's car. Mum wanted to talk to Sue, Dad wanted to talk to Donna, Mr. Nic wanted to talk to Rob, all the kids wanted to be together, and Briquette wanted to be with everyone.

So we set off: five kids, seven adults, one dog, and tons of food, PLUS hundreds of last-minute can't-possibly-survive-without-this things wedged into every tiny space. (I had the Monopoly digging into my neck, Danielle had a bag of ripe apricots that kept escaping over her shoulder, and Frank had Briquette under his feet.)

We stopped for a picnic. Danielle had a fight with Frank, so we all got back into our own cars—until we stopped for popsicles, then we all got into different cars again.

7
Through the Gate

We followed Old Jim's map (which turned out to be spot on) through the last town and on for twelve miles. Then we did a right-hand turn off the paved road, onto a dirt track. We bumped and bounced along, with the track getting rougher and rougher, until every bone in our bodies felt disengaged.

"Hope this is worth it!" said Dad.

"Hope the car doesn't fall to bits," said Frank.

"Hope *I* don't fall to bits," said Danielle.

"Hope Donna's all right," said Mum.

"Well, it was her idea in the first place," said Dad. "She wanted to get back to nature. Well, this is nature. Now keep your eyes open for the gate."

On and on we bumped, getting pretty cross and uncertain, when suddenly there was a gate on the left-hand side. It was rusty, bent, and mended with bits of wire. Nobody had been through that gate for a long time. Mr. Nic and I had to drag it open along the ground, across clumps of grass. Then, almost like it happens in the movies, an old man with a kelpie dog appeared from nowhere. Even though it was warm, he was wearing an extraordinary possum-skin vest. He wasn't smiling. He held up his hand in a stop signal.

"That's him," said Dad.

The old man looked at the three cars, sizing us up, deciding whether to cooperate or not. Donna heaved herself out and did the pregnant roll over to meet him. He watched her carefully.

"What is this?" whispered Dad. "Some sort of test we have to pass? Why can't we just buy a map and go somewhere normal!"

"Maps don't tell you the good spots. Just pipe down," said Mum.

Donna and Old Jim talked for a couple of minutes, then Donna waved for all of us to come over.

We squeezed ourselves out of the cars (the Monopoly, a roll of toilet paper, several apricots, and Briquette fell out with us), and gingerly we walked toward them. It was as if we might frighten him away.

"Pleased to meet you," said Mr. Nic. They shook leathery old hands.

Mr. Nic gazed around. "There used to be a railway station hereabouts, if I remember rightly," he said. (You could have fooled us. There was absolutely nothing but thick bush.)

"Yeah," said Old Jim, raising his bristly white eyebrows. "Now, how would you know about that?"

"Used to work for the railways," said Mr. Nic. "Long time

ago. The State Library had a service for readers in remote areas. I sent parcels of books up here once a month for years."

Old Jim cracked a smile. "Cracked" is the right word. His old walnut face changed, and the deep lines rearranged themselves into a smile! We all smiled at his smile.

"Well, I never!" he said. "They would've been fer me!" Old Jim took off his hat and scratched his head. "I was on me own most of the time. Read anything I could lay me hands on. Rode down to the station once a month to pick 'em up. Brown paper parcels tied up with string. Well, how about that!"

"What sort of books did they send you?" I asked, with visions of parcels arriving for me.

"Anything you wanted. Thrillers. Adventure. Animals. When I got onto a good writer, I read everything they'd written. Yeah, still use that string."

Donna could see these two old blokes would rabbit on all day, given half a chance.

"We're going to do some reading, too," she said with a smile, "but first we have to get there."

"Righty-o," said Old Jim. (Obviously, we had passed the test.) "Yeah, it's a lovely little spot on the Warrangalla. Only a mile or two farther down the valley. Ya drivin' across private property, but don't let that worry ya. It belonged to Old Man Rushton. He died last year," he said with a smile of satisfaction, as if he'd won a competition. "Nobody's been near the place since. Don't you go tellin' everyone about it, either."

We caught Briquette and squashed back into the cars. I had ". . . *brown paper packages tied up with string, these are a few of my favorite things . . .*" stuck in my head.

"I might visit ya sometime."

"Please do," said Donna, heaving herself into the van.

"Take it slowly!" called Old Jim, waving as we bumped past him.

"No other way to take it," said Dad.

8
A Wild Place

Our little convoy wound its way slowly down into a valley, lurching over rocks and tussocks. Trees brushed the sides of the car, and once we had to stop to drag a big branch off the track. Then we came to a wide, shallow ford. We leaned out the windows and got sprayed as the water whooshed away from the wheels. The adventure had begun!

"How will we know when we're there?" asked Danielle.

The cars strained up a steep slope and eased over the top. Then, on the other side, the bush opened out dramatically. We knew this was the spot. No doubt about it.

We drove down into the grassy clearing. Through the ancient river gum trees, we could see a wide curve of sparkling river, glittering in the sun as it flowed over rocks. On the downstream side, a ring of larger rocks seemed to frame the pool, and a magnificent forest rose up steeply on the far bank. To the left of the pool grew a tall stand of feathery poplars. As a final touch, a little breeze brushed the native grasses.

"Oh man!"

"Cool!"

"Magnificent!" said Rob.

We looked around.

"Just magnificent!"

More looking.

"Absolutely magnificent!"

"Stop saying 'magnificent' and help me out of this car," said Donna.

But that's how it felt. Magnificent.

Rob tried his cell phone. Nothing. The outside world was gone.

"I think we've driven into a wilderness poster," said Zev.

Then, as we all scrambled out, there came this creepy

Crreeiiïcraaaqasheshshe!!!

and a mighty branch thudded down from one of the gum trees by the river.

"Well, if that's how you feel, we'll go!" said Danielle.

"Why did it do that?" asked Cass.

"When the load becomes too great for the tree to support, it drops a branch," said Sue.

"Look it up in *What Branch Falling Down Is That?*" said Rob.

"Don't put your tent under a tree," said Mum.

It was a strong reminder that we were in a wild place, so two minutes after arriving, we got the "wild place" lecture, which included snakes, going off on your own, sunscreen, drinking plenty of water, etc., etc., etc.

The first thing we checked out was the river—the wondrous wide pool with the rocky beach. Then we scrambled around the corner to where it babbled on downstream, through smooth sculpted rocks.

"Can we drink straight from it, like animals?" asked Cass.

"Well, if the water up here's polluted, we're in real trouble," said Dad.

Briquette was racing in circles. "Mad dog!" yelled Zev. "She's doing a pelter!"

"This is absolutely so cool," said Danielle, doing a handstand.

"And you wanted mini golf and trampolines!" said Dad.

"Fab-ee-yoo-lus!"

"I'm going for a swim!"

Putting up the Big Top was a major operation, and very funny! As Rob, Zev, and I lugged it from the van, the elastic in Zev's shorts gave out. "My pants are falling down inside the opera!" he sang. "They are now below the reproductive organs." Then we couldn't find the front of the tent.

For the final touch, we unrolled the carpet. Te-dah! You could tell it had been very bright by two vivid patches, once covered by furniture. Although mostly threadbare, it had a rich magic look.

"The carpet Aladdins it," said Cass.

As long as I live, I'll never forget knitting and playing Spoons on that carpet.

The next funny thing was the Lilo blower-upper. It made the most fantastically disgusting rude fart noise, which came from one tent after another and gave Frank a giggling fit.

Zev, Danielle, and I had Lilos, Frank had a Therm-a-Rest, and Cass had a sponge roll. Everyone was envious of Rob and Donna's new velour Lilo.

"The Rolls-Royce of Lilos," said Donna as she lay there watching us slave away.

In the tent that night, Frank asked, "Is this wilderness? It doesn't seem like wilderness."

"That's because we're all here together," said Danielle. "If you were here alone, it'd be mega-wilderness."

"How was that branch falling?" said Zev.

"That reminds me," I warned everyone, "Danielle is a wild sleeper."

"Zev, make your hair sparklify!" said Cass.

The sparks danced out of his hair that night—like fireworks.

"Must be better on vacations," said Frank.

"I'm going to sleep now," said Danielle. "Last one in for a swim tomorrow's a monkey's uncle."

Dear God,
Thank you
Henni

I woke up in the night and heard a sound that I thought was rain. I stuck my hand outside . . . nothing. It was just the low soothing murmur of the river.

Later, I woke up in the moonlight as a flurry of wind swept through the treetops. Night birds were calling to each other.

9
We're Never Leaving

It was very early next morning when I woke and suddenly remembered where we were. I peeped through the tent flap to see if it was real, and wriggled halfway out. Of all the billions of leaves in the bush, not one of them stirred. Golden light filled the clearing, and the crazy twisted gum branches were silhouetted against the sky.

The birds were making an incredible racket as if they were all cheering for their team, nonstop, at the bird grand final. Behind all this was the steady burble of the river flowing over rocks.

I watched a cockatoo and a pair of magpies fighting a duel. The cocky must have trespassed into their airspace, and the magpies were going for him like Darth Vader's Tie Fighters. Eventually they chased the cocky away.

Whipbirds cracked their whips, and a funny alarm-clock bird sang its one note—*da da da da . . . da da da da . . . da da da da. . . .*

All the other tents were zipped up. No one was astir. Feeling incredibly happy, I wriggled down into my sleeping bag and went back to sleep.

First one kookaburra started laughing, then he set the others off. They chortled and cackled for ages in the closest gum tree.

"Those kookaburras have the best sense of humor I've ever struck in a bird," called a sleepy voice from Mr. Nic's tent.

"Wish they'd share the joke," said Tibor.

Rob unfolded himself out of the yellow tent, stretched and scratched in half a dozen places, then strode to the fire.

"Did anybody remember to bring matches?"

"I did!" "We did!" "In the blue box." "Yep!" came voices from every tent.

We had fifteen boxes of matches!

By the time everyone was awake, Rob had lit the fire, carted up two buckets of water from the river, put a pot on for tea, and found the bread and eggs and bacon and the tennis-racket-sized frying pan.

"My pillow migrates," said Danielle, punching it hard. She had ended up sleeping on the groundsheet.

"My Lilo is a very lie-low," said Zev.

"How low can you go?"

"It's flat!"

"That's low!"

"With camping you get toughened," said Danielle. "The first night's bad because it's all strange, then the second night's good because you're tired."

Cass took ages to wake up. She sat in her sleeping bag and groaned, and rubbed her eyes, and stared nowhere, like a spaced-out zombie. "Numbeling," she calls it.

Mr. Nic came backward out of his little tent, like a strange old stick insect emerging from its cocoon. For the first time, we saw his legs. It was quite a shock. They were porridge-colored twigs. They stuck out of his floppy khaki shorts, which were held up by a leather belt.

"Don't go near a goanna in that outfit," said Dad.

Mr. Nic chuckled and explained to Frank how goannas run up the closest thing.

Danielle emerged with her hair like a bird's nest. She smoothed down both sides roughly at the front with her hands.

"Go and do your hair," said Mum.

"I have," said Danielle, and it was such a funny lie she got away with it.

"I wouldn't worry," laughed Tibor, watching Danielle and Cass practicing handstands. "You see more of her feet than her face."

"'Start your day with the goodness of sunshine,'" read Zev, shoveling in his breakfast.

". . . and a bucket of sugar," goes Rob.

"'Delicious frosted flakes of corn.'"

". . . and a bucket of sugar."

"'Three thousand essential vitamins and iron bars.'"

". . . and a bucket of sugar," goes Rob.

"Don't you wish you were back on your swivel chair at the computer, Tibor?" Dad poured second cups of tea all around.

"I'm winding down so much I'll need retraining," said Tibor, who has his own computer business and would have to retrain himself.

A cheeky crimson rosella picked up our stray corn flakes, and a flycatcher flew aerobatics after our insects.

That first day we did nothing, just swam, lay around, pottered, set up camp, and marveled at our luck.

"We're never leaving here," said Mum.

"We'll have babies and grow vegetables. You men can go hunting and fishing," said Donna.

"We'll never go to school," said Danielle.

"We'll just play all day," said Frank.

One of our top priorities was the making of the toilet. Mr. Nic and Rob chose a secluded spot, well away from the river, and they dug the hole. To make it more private, although you couldn't see it from the camp, Rob rigged up a hessian screen.

Dad thought it was so artistic he called it the Arts Council Grant Sculpture. It was very neat, with a proper shovel, but even so the flies buzzed around like kids at an arcade.

Briquette was deliriously free to do whatever she wanted, *except* get into the food boxes (a lesson she learned in the first hour). She had her rug under the yellow tent fly on Rob's side, and a cool clear river to drink from, and she could be with her favorite humans all the time.

Then Briquette found extra bliss somewhere on the riverbank. Just as we were chomping into the last-of-the-Christmas-ham sandwiches in the last-of-the-spongy-white bread, up trots Briquette with something in her mouth.

"Oh, Briquette! You're *disgusting*!"

"What is it?"

"What's she got?"

"The *disgustingest* smelly old hoof."

"*Briquette!*" Rob wrestled it out of her mouth. "You and your disgusting hoof—hoof it!" And with a mighty throw, he flung it way off into the bush, then washed his hands and got back to his sandwich.

"These mince pies are absolutely yummy, Sue," said Dad.

"Purchased by hand," said Sue, with a TV-mum smile.

We had a boat race with the aluminum pie plates. Mine kept sinking. The trick was to launch your little boat in just the right part of the river, where the current was strongest. There was a bit of a scare when Frank chased his boat out into deep water and started to be carried down the river. I managed to grab him.

I didn't think it was *that* serious, but Frank was trembly, and the grown-ups freaked right out. Dad saw it all in Technicolor detail. Donna was megaworried. That's when we got the Don't Stress Donna lecture. This was a major lecture punctuated with "Do you understands?" and "We mean its!" and "Can we trust yous?" After which, we invented the Don't Stress Donna secret sign.

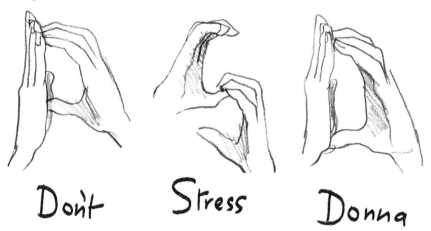

Don't Stress Donna

The result was the first of Tibor's rope tricks. He swam across the river with a long piece of rope, which he tied to a tree on each bank with a very professional-looking knot. This solved the problem. If you were swept away, all you had to do was catch the rope and pull yourself to shallow water.

The stand of poplar trees on the riverbank, to the left of our beach, was like a cool leafy cathedral. In the hottest part of the day, we took our picnic blankets, books, pillows, and magazines to this shady spot and flopped. We called it the Reading Room.

"You look like a litter of puppies," said Sue, settling into her *Epicure* magazine. Mum read us a bit of Roald Dahl's *Matilda* each day, and even Dad put down his financial newspaper and listened. Mum used a gum leaf for a bookmark.

Briquette broke the serenity. Yes. You've guessed it . . . the hoof!

Rob wrenched it out of her mouth again and marched off into the bush. "Hang on to that dog, will you."

Briquette couldn't understand why we didn't like her magnificent hoof.

Rob returned a bit later. "We've seen the last of that!"

Later, in the Big Top, in the dark, we had an in-depth conversation about how dogs are different from humans.

"If Cass was Briquette, and we kept taking her hoof away, she would slather and blather and flap around like a chicken with its head chopped off."

"What about if Danielle was Briquette?"

"I'd bite!" she said, quick as a flash.

"What about you, Henni? I know," said Zev. "You'd think

about it for ages, then go away and write about how the hoof was feeling!" (Ho ho ho! Very funny!)

"Zev, if someone took your hoof, you'd say, 'Now, why did they do that? I was doing electrical experiments on it, but now I will do electrical experiments on them.'" (Actually, Zev would never hurt anyone.)

"Frank would yell, 'They've taken my hoof and I want it back!'"

But Briquette still loves us, even though we take her hoof. No grudges.

"Maybe she hasn't got a memory," said Zev.

"She has *so* got a memory," said Frank.

10
Skinny-dipping, or Free Willies II

(This was the day we got sunburned.)

Skinny-dipping happened in order of age. Frank was the first one, because he couldn't find his bathing suit. (Thank you, Danielle, for keeping our tent so clean and tidy.)

Then Cass *dared* Danielle, so that was an easy one.

"It's fantastic!" Danielle screeched. "So cool! And you don't have to find your bathing suit and put it on and hang it up and all that bothery stuff."

She swam over to the other side, shouting, "It's warm. It's freezing. It's freezing. It's warm!" as she glided through the patches of water. "It's icy when you put your feet down. Here's a really cold patch."

"Hey, guys! I'm skinshinning!" yelled Cass, standing on a rock, waving her suit. Then she flung it onto the bank.

I was a bit embarrassed at first, and sort of hid myself in the water, but it was especially luxurious for me because I get eczema from chlorinated pools. I loved the cool slippery fish feeling, so mermaidy and free.

"Free Willie!" yelled Zev, doing a bomb from a rock.

Only two adults went skinny-dipping, and they were quite private about it. Not like us.

It was thirty-five steps down the bank from the Big Top to the pool. The large rounded rocks to one side we called the Government Rocks, because the parents looked like tribal elders when they sat there. Then upstream there was a pointed rock we called Bird Poo Island, where a couple of herons liked to do business.

The river flowed smoothly—deep, dark, and cool—near the far side. The current was strong. Even if you swam full bore, you didn't get anywhere, and yet you could hardly tell it was moving except for the leaves and sticks it carried along.

A lizard had a favorite log on the far side, where he lay in the sun, perfectly camouflaged.

"Where is he? I can't see him," said Frank.

"See where that tree is, near the rock?" said Cass.

"Which tree near which rock? There's millions of trees and rocks."

"He's gone now."

The pool was wonderful for Donna. She slipped in and dreamed around by herself. Instead of being so big and heavy with Baby Watermelon, she floated in the delicious water. Rob called her the great white whale. The rest of the time she pottered around botanicalizing, or lounged with her thriller. Everything she did was in slow motion.

"Donna looks very healthy," said Mum.

"Mmm, sort of soft and furry at the edges," said Cass.

We laughed.

Cass made a rock shop selling—you guessed it—rocks! The interesting shapes and the good skimmers were the most expensive. Then Danielle discovered you could draw on some rocks with other rocks, so she had a cell phone and clock rock shop.

Lucky Frank found a rare treasure—a perfect heart-shaped rock. He named it the Heart of the Pool, and we had to pay a gum nut to see it in its museum.

I had a paint shop with all the different-colored clays.

We decorated each other with the clay, like for an initiation, and we spiked up Zev's hair.

Then someone (probably Cass or Danielle) invented a game called Pop Bango. What happens is that one person is It, and they call out instructions, like "Scissors! Ballet dancer! Victory

Scissors

Submarine

Karate kick

Spaz-attack

Ballerina

Dog's ears

sign!" Then everyone else has to do a handstand in the river, and make scissors, ballet dancer, or whatever, with their legs. The adults thought it was so funny they came down and watched; then they took over the calling and judging.

After dark, they joined in our game of Spotlight, too. It's more fun if there's more people. Mr. Nic hardly moved from behind his bush. No wonder he survived the war. I was really proud of Mum. She very nearly got home.

"Now we play hospital," said Dad, dabbing the blood from a scratch on his leg. We were all a bit wrecked, one way or another.

It was cool that night.

"I've got my sunburn to keep me warm," said Zev.

11
Cool Pool Days

"The worst thing," said Mr. Nic, "is a sunburned bottom!"

It must have been the fresh air and the bare legs, he was so lively. He did little jigs and wanted us to play-fight.

"I remember an epic sunburn," said Mum. "My brother peeled a sheet of skin from my back the size of a small envelope." (My sensible mum got sunburned?!)

Rob became quite inspired. Every now and then he came out with a scrap of poetry or a bit of a song. When he works, he sometimes sings, but the poetry was a real surprise. *We love to pamper the camper, who carries an oversized hamper,*" he spouted to Donna, then he did a little hippy dance around her and sang, "*I believe in miracles. Where you from, you sexy thing?*"

The adults were getting on well, though I know Dad sometimes annoys Rob because he wants to organize everything, and Rob annoys Dad because he doesn't want to be organized.

Tibor was irritated by the messy kitchen boxes, so he set out to design the perfect chuck wagon. When Tibor has a project in mind, he doesn't say anything, just stooges around collecting what he needs, like a bird making a nest.

Then he put the chuck wagon idea aside and watched us in

the pool. He borrowed my goggles and checked out underwater obstacles where the big tree leaned out over the water. Then he stood on a cooler and asked Danielle to climb up on his shoulders and throw a rope over the branch over the pool. A knot slipped tight, securing it at the top; then he tied a stick to the bottom. Finally, Tibor climbed high on the bank, jumped, swung right out over the pool, and did a mighty bomb into the deep water.

"Wicked!"

The first time you did it, you left your stomach in midair for a second. We did bellywhackers, pindrops, and bombs. We yelled as we swung and screamed as we dropped.

"You're in and out of that water like tea bags in a cuppa tea," said Mr. Nic.

At Donna's request, Tibor's next project was a perfect miniature chest of drawers made by lashing twelve matchboxes together with thin red string. We kept our small treasures in it.

So the days slid away. The sun came up and the sun went down, and we more or less went up and down with it. Everything was what it was. Wood was wood, water was water, stones were stones, and fun was fun.

The weather was perfect for the first few days; then it grew steadily hotter. There were a couple of conversations about what we would do if a bush fire came through, and we were always extra-careful about our cooking fire. But as things turned out, fire certainly was not the problem.

We went for bushwalks—bushbashing really—along animal tracks. We went back to the ford and fossicked around there. We made a useful little raft, the size of a small tray, from plastic containers and bottles, then floated our shoes and hats to the other side of the river, swam across, and explored the far bank.

We found the ruins of an old house (well, actually about five bricks and a patch of ivy, but you could see where the house used to be) and a plum tree laden with ripe plums. Cass found the second best of our treasures: the little china foot.

We were sure it was Alice in Wonderland's foot.

Cass was the best treasure-hunter, which was annoying because she never seemed to *look*. Too busy standing on her hands. She says she's got "finding eyes."

We returned to camp with our hats full of plums. Chief chef Sue groaned. "When we've eaten the pineapple and the last of the mangoes and all the food we *have* to eat, *then* we'll start on the plums."

Tibor completed his masterpiece.

"See, Henni!" he said. "I *did* have the kitchen sink in my rope bag!"

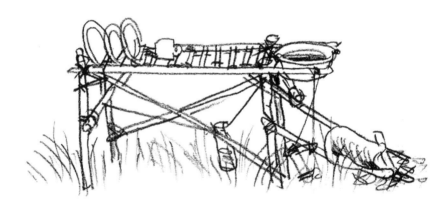

12
A Miss Dippy Flip-Top Disappears

That night, Danielle woke us all up. She flung her arms and legs around, tossing and turning and saying very clearly, as if she was petrified, "You go back in there! You go back in there!" Then next morning, she said, "Slept like a log. Did anybody have any dreams?"

Mr. Nic told us he had a dream where he said to himself, "My word, I'm sleeping well!" Every morning when he scrambled out of his little cocoon tent, he used to say, "If I was any fitter, I'd be dangerous!"

The first human sound of the morning was not a tiny lawn mower or a massive wasp but Rob's electric shaver chewing at his chin. Next came the cracking of sticks as someone started the fire for the day. Then the clink of plates and frying pans, scrumbling in food boxes, quiet adult talking and chuckling about something, and all the time the birds and the quiet burble of the river.

We walked and talked with the walkie-talkie, but we had to take it in turns. One of our best games out of the water was Dis (short for Disappeared). There were great places to hide. It was about the fifth game when Danielle vanished—completely evaporated. Everyone else had been found. Zev, who was It,

53

searched and searched, then everyone started looking—parents, too—even in stupid places, like under Donna!

"Miss Dippy Flip-Top's totally flipped this time!" said Tibor.

"Gone forever?"

"Hope so," said Sue loudly.

"Yeah. She's a boring old rotten egg. Always doing spaz attacks. Besides, I'm sick of looking at her feet all the time," said Rob. (The loud rude insult technique usually works.)

We looked EVERYWHERE!

"She's gone into hanky-panky land," said Cass.

"Danielle's found the best hiding place in the Northern Atmosphere," said Frank.

"You mean the Southern Hemisphere."

"Briquette, find Danielle! Find Danielle! Fetch!" commanded Frank.

Briquette galloped away so confidently we all galloped after her. Then she came loping out from behind a tree with something in her mouth.

"Oh *no!* The dreaded hoof!"

"I reckon she's gone outside the boundary of the game," said Zev as we searched down by the river. "Danielle, you're cheating!" he yelled at the top of his lungs.

"No I wasn't!" sang Danielle, right behind us, doing an I'm-a-smartie cartwheel. "I was there *all the time.* I heard *every* word you said. Test me."

Then Cass noticed Donna on her lounge chair, grinning like a Cheshire cat.

"Donna knows!"

But no matter how we threatened with torture, bribed with gummy bears, or pleaded on bended knees, Donna wouldn't tell us the hiding spot.

13
Possums? Fairies?

"I heard noises last night," said Frank.

He was changing into his pajamas absentmindedly by the fire. He took off the pajama top he had just put on, dropped it on the ground, then picked it up and put it back on again.

"What sort of noises? Snoring? Farting? Hoof-chewing?"

"Rummaging noises, with plastic bag wrinklings, and then crackling sticks and leaves, like from footprints."

"You mean footsteps."

"Possums!" said Dad, inspecting his burned marshmallow. "Possums for sure! No matter what it sounds like, it's possums. I've heard possums sound like machine guns, explosions, a car crash, a pub brawl, a dying cow, but mostly they sound like robbers or murderers coming to get you."

"I remember once we'd just come back from a week's vacation," said Rob. "Opened the door, and the place was wrecked! 'Vandals have broken in and trashed the place,' we said. 'Call the cops!' Black stuff everywhere, things broken, curtains ripped, mega mess. Then I went to take something out of the saucepan cupboard and there's this little possum face peering out at me. He'd fallen down the chimney and couldn't get out! Did enough damage for a whole gang!"

Then the adults told their most nightmarish possum stories, which all ended with "But it was only *a possum!*" Then Rob made up a shaggy dog story which ended with "But it wasn't a possum, it was only a ghost!"

The subject jumped like a grass fire from possums, to how noisy the frogs were, to being giddy, to hitting your head, to hospital food, to how people like their eggs cooked, to eating kidneys, to football injuries, to names for Baby Football (Donna was sure it was a boy), etc., etc., etc. You know how it goes.

"Who pinched the last of those coconut cookies?" asked Cass, rummaging.

"Didn't know we had any left."

"I stashed them yesterday in the box with the chopping board, under the cereal."

"Well, too bad. Somebody's eaten them."

"You should have had some yesterday when everybody else did."

"I'd just chomped into a new gum."

"The fairies took 'em," said Danielle.

Frank was leaning back against Rob, twiddling Donna's hair. "Mum, do you believe in fairies?" he asked.

"I tried to," said Donna, "but they never quite worked for me. We didn't have a potting shed at the bottom of the garden,

57

or a stile near a dell, or those mushrooms with spots that fairies like to sit on. Fairies seemed too pretty and delicate for our creeks and paddocks and gum trees."

"Haven't we got fairies?" asked Frank, worried that we'd missed out on something.

"We could invent some," said Zev.

"No," said Cass. "You can't just invent things like that. They have to be old and sort of language-worn, like the round stones in the river."

"I think the spirits here would be strong," said Danielle. "Not flitty fairies with wimpy wands and fairy dust."

"The Aborigines have rock-dwellers and other spirits like that," said Zev.

In the flickering firelight, I could almost imagine something lurking in the shadows behind us.

Later, when the last coals were settling in the fire, and we were sliding down into our sleeping bags, Frank said quietly, "I don't believe in fairies, and it wasn't a possum."

"You and your noises!" said Danielle.

"Wake me up next time," I said to him, and the last thing I remembered before dropping off to sleep was feeling for the little black flashlight under my pillow.

14
Catching the Possum

The following day was New Year's Eve. After dusk, when the stars came out, we celebrated by hiking back along the track, listening to the noises of the night.

"It's going to be a very eventful new year," said Rob, "with babies and junior high school."

An owl hooted twice.

"He doesn't care two hoots!" said Mr. Nic. He is *so* corny.

"Oh, *look!*" Rob was excited. "Sugar gliders! Wondrous little things. This is their landing patch. See the scratches?" He shone the flashlight up the trunk of the gum. Right on cue, a little possum slapped against the tree and scampered off. Rob found another possum and traced the path of its flight with the flashlight. It was amazing to see these tiny furballs make kites of themselves and leap from tree to tree.

"Why do they do it?"

"For kicks. They're like kids on skateboards. They love it. And it makes them tricky for other animals to catch."

Rob's flashlight swept round the dark bush, then Cass suddenly squeaked as if she'd been pinched.

"I saw somebody!" Her face was white. She looked all wobbly.

"I just saw somebody! Behind that tree! A hairy man!"

We caught her fear.

"I wasn't imagining it. I definitely, definitely saw somebody," said Cass.

Rob immediately went over and shone his flashlight all around. *"Hello? Who's there?"* No one. Not a sign. Nothing.

The adults went into cooing quieting mode.

"We're a long way from anywhere. Who'd be spying on us? What would they want with us? There's nothing to steal. We don't have any secrets."

Then they tried the humorous approach. "Does anybody have a nuclear bomb in their bag?"

"Could've been Old Jim. He said he'd visit us."

"No, it wasn't Old Jim. It wasn't his shape."

"Too much scary possum talk."

"Not enough sleep!"

"You saw something, Cass, and we don't know what it was, but I really don't think it would be a person," said Sue. "Might be a kangaroo looking like a person."

Later, trying to sleep, we talked about it for ages.

"Maybe you're right, Frank," said Cass. "Maybe someone has been stealing our food."

Next morning we went through the kitchen boxes and counted

all the stuff we thought might be disappearing, especially things in crinkly packets.

"How many 2 Minute Noodles?"

"Twenty-two 2 Minute Noodles."

"How many Weetabix? Cookies? Etc., etc., etc. Okay. We count them again tomorrow."

"You taking inventory?" asked Mum.

"What's that?"

"Where you count up all your stock."

"We're seeing if a possum's taking stuff," I said.

"They're so *positive* it's possums," said Danielle.

The following morning: twenty-*one* 2 Minute Noodles! And four Weetabix gone!

"A little bit of this and a little bit of that," said Zev.

"Tonight we'll take it in turns to watch, like they do on ships," said Zev. "First Danielle, then Cass, me, Hen, and Frank. Two hours each."

Danielle found a suitable stick.

"Then what? Follow them? Arrest them? What if they're dangerous? What if it's desperate? An evil spirit with a deadly weapon?" The others were churning themselves into total terror.

"Earth to Dan, Cass, and Frank!" said Zev. "Weetabix and 2 Minute Noodles! I'll distract; Hen, you shine the flashlight; Cass, you yell for the parents; and Dan, you be ready with the stick."

It was Cass who shook me awake, so terrified she couldn't make a sound.

A large dark figure was going through the kitchen boxes. Zev slipped out, and next thing—sparks appeared to fly out of the bucket on the kitchen table.

The figure froze. I snapped the flashlight on its face. "Oh *no!*" "It's HEAP!"

In that split second, the vacation changed.

Remember Heap, from Donna's work? Well, Heap was this dumb kid who wandered between his mum and his dad, stinking of cigarettes and running into stupid trouble—like being caught on a tram without a ticket, and pinching a liter of milk. At school he wasn't bad, but he couldn't read, so he didn't learn much. His mother chucked him out, so sometimes he lived with his grandmother. He was older than us, and as pierced as a pincushion.

He stayed with Donna and Rob for a bit, and we tried to include him in our games, but he was hopeless and the games just died. He used to laugh at our jokes, pretending to understand—but he just never got it. One thing he was good at was sleeping. He said his father trained him to sleep, with beer.

I think Donna was the only one who had ever been kind to him. For a little while, he came good, and motored along as if Donna had got him into gear. He even had what Rob called "a near-work experience," but it didn't stick. He always slouched and sort of shuffled around. When he was staying with Rob and Donna, Mum said she kept wanting to make him stand straight and pick up his feet. But who cares about posture if you haven't got a mum or dad?

Donna liked him. She saw something in him that we didn't. She tried hard, but could never find a place where his strange shape would fit in.

I was totally *amazed* that Heap had found us in this secluded spot. Maybe he wasn't such a dead loss. He must have been desperate to have walked so far alone, following our tracks. He was wearing a dirty stained T-shirt that said LIVE ON THE EDGE— NO RULES, and black sweatpants with rips in the knees. His hair was long, knotted, and cavemanish, so he looked as if he didn't have a neck.

"What, in the whole history of the universe, are you doing here, Heap?" said Zev, steering him away from the tents.

"I want Donna to help me."

We groaned inside, but not spitfire Danielle. She blurted straight out, "Donna picked this vacation because she wanted to be quiet and peaceful and totally away from everybody—especially people like you! So GO AWAY!"

Boy! We *were* all wishing he wasn't there, but Danielle was so blunt and rude. Cass was shocked. Even Heap, who never reacted to anything much, looked more downtrodden than ever.

"What's wrong?" I asked. Danielle glared at me like a fighting rooster.

Heap slumped onto a rock and droned out the whole sorry story: he'd skipped some school (the special school Donna spent ages getting him into) because kids were picking on him, then he had another fight with his mum—

"*Typical!*" snapped Danielle—and his mum told him to get lost and go to his dad, but his dad had moved—"*Typical!*"—so Heap had been sleeping in the garage of an empty house, which was better than the box under the bridge, then for a while he'd slept on the trains in the daytime, then met these kids who used to hang around this shopping center snatching purses—"*Typical!*"—and if they saw an open door, they just walked in, grabbed what they could, and walked out, and then they'd have a feed, and they were buying drugs cheap, but Heap said he never did—"*Typical!*"—"Shut up, Danielle. That's not helping."—and he never stole nothing—

I could just imagine him trailing along with those idiot kids, laughing at their stupid jokes. He would've stuck to them, because somehow Heap sticks to you like dog poo deep in the pattern on the sole of your shoe.

He said it was Christmas and he was hungry and the kids told him to wait while they went into this shop. He didn't know this kid had a knife. The bloke in the shop had a gun and shot one of the kids in the leg, and Heap ran away, but he was sure the cops were looking for him — *"Typical!"*

And now he was our problem!

Dear God, Why do we have to have Heap? He wants Donna! Couldn't this be a happy holiday without complications? They say you've got a plan for us all but does Heap *have* to be in *OUR* plan? Couldn't he have a path of his own? Danielle's going off her head at him. Please God, PLEASE find another path for Heap. Yours in desperation.
Henni

"I want to talk to Donna," said Heap.

"You can't," said Danielle, giving us a fierce Don't Stress Donna signal.

"Where are you living?"

"In the bush on the other side of the river."

"In a tent?"

"Got a sleeping bag and a groundsheet."

"And you're nicking food off us."

"S'pose so."

"Aren't you scared?"

"Nah. I feel safe. No one's pinching my stuff. No one's pissing on me in the night."

We thought about that one for a bit.

"What do you do all day?" said Cass.

"Walk around. Watch you guys."

"Yeah? Even skinny-dipping?"

He grinned.

"You're a perv!" said Danielle.

"How did you find us?" said Zev.

"Everybody on Stella Street knew you were camping up here. I asked a lady in the grocery in the last town, and she told me you were going somewhere off the road. Took me a couple of days to find the turnoff, hitching up and down. I want to talk to Donna."

We needed time to think.

"Not now," I said.

"*Never!*" said Danielle.

"What can Donna do, Heap?" said Zev.

"Tell the cops that I wasn't part of the gang and nothing was my fault."

"Do you think she's going to jump in the car instantly and drive all the way to Melbourne to do that?"

"Go tell 'em yourself," said Danielle.

"They wouldn't believe me," said Heap.

She couldn't reply to that because from our experience it was true.

"Heap, Donna's going to have a *baby*. She's left work. *You* were her *work*. Now get lost! GO AWAY!" said Danielle.

He was pathetic, but determined. I stalled.

"Look," I said, "if you *promise* to stay on your side of the river, we'll get food for you. Better food. Cooked food. Okay?"

"When can I see Donna?"

"We'll talk about it later."

Suddenly he seemed quite happy. For him it was progress, I guess.

"You know those two big rocks either side of the river, downstream? They're the Talk Rocks. We'll meet you there after breakfast tomorrow morning and throw the food over."

Looking back, we should have told somebody (but not Donna) about Heap. They would have sorted something out. But we wanted the vacation to be just us. Donna and Rob probably *would* have driven back with him. Or else he'd have stayed with us. Which was worse?

Danielle was in a raging temper. "You are so *stupid*, Hen! If we *help* him, he'll *stay*!" she roared. "You always think you're so *right*, Miss Well-brought-up Goody-goody. Well, I'll *make* him go away! Let him get his own life!"

Then I saw Cass grin at Danielle. I was really hurt.

"*Stop* it!" Zev cut in. "Hen's right—we had to do something."

So, after the first fight of the vacation, we took on the problem of Heap. We nicked food and threw it over the river to him in an ice cream container. Secretly I hoped, like the others, the bush would be too rough for him and he'd disappear back to town. But also, without knowing it, I began to admire how he could survive.

"Heap," I yelled, "when you go, put a stone on your Talk Rock. That will be the sign that you've left, and then we won't worry about you."

"You're pathetic!" said Danielle.

"You kids are eating like horses," said Sue. "Must be all the fresh air."

"Going through a growing jag," said Tibor.

We all asked for big helpings and passed around the ice cream container when no one was looking. Everyone had to put in something for Heap.

"I'm staaaaarving," Danielle said, helping herself to three fat sausages.

"What a little guts!" said Dad.

Actually, Danielle *was* ravenous and she *did* want to eat it all herself. She passed the container straight on. I gave her a jab in the ribs that said we *all* had to put food in.

Ever tried to flip spaghetti off your plate into an ice cream container on your lap, without being noticed?

15
A Lot of Swearing

Mum is a quiet person—not shy, but a thinking, watching type. Sometimes, while Dad's organizing something, Mum just goes and does it. She very, very rarely gets cross, but Mum blew a fuse when Danielle couldn't find her hat.

"No hat, no walk!"

So we left Danielle scrabbling through the mess in the Big Top.

We were dawdling along behind the adults, talking about how Heap looked a bit happier that morning, and waiting for Danielle to catch up, when suddenly she came pounding toward us, all flustered, blustered, and urgent.

"Wait . . . for me . . . wait . . ." She was so out of breath she could hardly talk. "I was in the tent . . . when I heard the sound of a car! . . . I thought it was the police looking . . . for Heap, and I was scared, so I hid in the secret spot.

"Well, the car drove up close . . . then the engine stopped and doors slammed . . . and there was a man so *angry* at our camp!" said Danielle, eyes wide. "He swore and swore like anything."

"Why?"

"Because of where we're camped. I think we mucked up his plans, or something. He didn't say, 'This is my land.' He just went on about how 'Nobody knows about this place. Nobody comes here! How did they find it?' as if we were the biggest bit of bad luck since the Second World War.

"And there was a snivelly one who was sucking up to the angry one, the boss, and a third one who hardly said anything. I think he was younger."

"Wow! Then what happened?"

"They walked around saying, 'What a mess, and look at all this bloody junk from the city.' Things like 'My God, they brought everything.' He was so angry. And 'We can't do a thing with them here.' Then he said 'Fiddleback,' or something like that. I remember that word. Definitely fiddleback—like it was a thing. And Thommo's dozer."

"Are you sure it wasn't the cops?"

"Absolutely!"

"When he went into our tent, he said, 'They've even got bloody carpet in here!'

"Then they walked off, and when their voices were far away, I looked out and they were going through the trees, down beside the river."

"Did you follow them?"

"No, I came straight here to tell you guys."

"Shh!" said Zev, listening urgently. "Shut up!"

Very faintly, in our silence and through the birdcalls, we could hear the unmistakable chop, chop of an ax!

Then it stopped.

"That was—"

"Shhhh!" We froze and listened. Nothing, just the birds and the breeze in the treetops.

"Cutting something down!" whispered Frank.

"Not enough chopping for a tree," said Cass.

"Let's go back!"

"The parents will be way ahead by now," said Zev. "I'll tell them we've gone back to Danielle. Will I say about the men?"

"Yes," I said.

Contrary Danielle glared at me. "*NO!*" she snapped. "Not yet!" I guess this was her show. I didn't argue.

Zev raced ahead, while we thundered back like a herd of elephants. Just when we were close enough to sneak, we heard the car driving off.

"Oh, bumsocks!" said Cass.

Zev came pounding up as if he'd just run a marathon. "Did you see 'em?"

"Just missed them! The beggar runts!" said Cass.

16
Place of Spirits

We picked our way along the riverbank, searching high and low for something with cuts in it. We're usually good at that sort of thing, but the trouble was we didn't know what we were looking for.

"Three men. You'd reckon it would be easy to see where they went," said Zev.

"They *sounded* big," said Danielle.

We searched for snapped branches and bootprints. Zev was up front. "Yuuukk! I think we've gone the wrong way."

"Why?"

"I just walked straight into a spider's web! Urgghhh. Copped it full in the face!"

We came to a creek that flowed into the river. It wasn't deep, but there were no stepping-stones.

"I'm going to look on the other side." Zev took off his shoes and paddled over. "Can't see anything! This water's freezing."

"Well, they couldn't cross the river here. They either crossed the creek or went along it."

"Hey! Up here!" yelled Cass. "A footprint . . . I think."

So we pushed our way up the little creek, which got fernier

and more slippery with every step. Just as well Briquette was with the adults. We would have had to carry her.

The trees were different—taller, and their branches seemed to be high up. The ground was soft and sinky, and there was moss on every rock and tree trunk. Plants were growing up through other plants. It was a cool, dark growing place, completely different from the dry bush all around. It felt very, very old.

"This is a place of spirits, for sure," said Zev.

Fern fronds sprouted above us, like huge feather dusters on tall hairy trunks.

"The sun doesn't reach down here."

"This is rain forest," I said.

"It's not raining," said Frank.

"Primitive ancient rain forest."

"What if a dinosaur bends his head down and peers at us?" said Danielle.

"Isn't it amazing?"

We clambered over fallen logs and pushed through giant ferns.

"It's so beautiful, so green."

"Wouldn't Donna love this place!" said Danielle.

"You can say that again," I said.

"Wouldn't Donna love this place." We were nearly friends again.

Zev was somewhere up ahead. "Oh boy, is this wet, or what? Really oozy. Whoops. Nearly lost my boot. Think I'll come back."

"Look at *this* tree," said Cass, "it's *humongous!* That is the biggest tree I have ever seen in all my live-long life!"

"We could be the first people to ever come here," said Frank.

"What about the Aborigines?"

"What about those men?" said Cass.

We'd forgotten that we were looking for something.

"Hey, I *found* it!" yelled Zev from the other side of the tree.

We raced around to see. And there, about waist-high up the mighty trunk, a chip had been cut out.

"Oh no!"

"It looks so *wrong.* So *stupid,*" said Danielle.

We studied the new scar—an awful sign of man in this ancient place.

"*Why* did they do that?"

"To take a sample? To test it? Like if it's got a disease?"

"To see what sort of a tree it is?"

"No, they can see that by looking at the leaves and bark and stuff."

"To find out something about its insides."

"Must have been a sharp ax," said Zev. "Look how clean the cuts are."

"A scientific experiment?"

"No way," said Danielle. "They weren't scientists."

We sat on a fallen log on the other side of the scar.

"Do you think they want to cut the tree down?"

"No. They wouldn't . . . would they?"

"Oh yeah?" said Cass.

"Mum wouldn't like that!" said Frank.

"You can bet your gumboots she wouldn't!" said Danielle.

We tried to talk about it on the way back to camp, but it's hard when you're scrambling through the bush in single file. So we decided to discuss it in the Big Top, over a game of Spoons, with a tube of sweetened condensed milk to help us think.

The game conked out, because you can't talk when you play Spoons, and you need both hands free, which you haven't got if you're licking condensed milk off your finger.

We felt glum. First Heap—that was bad enough—and now these rotten men! We couldn't believe that anybody would touch that valley. Besides, how would they get the trees out?

"Drat this," said Danielle. "I'm off for a dip."

"Wait a sec," said Zev. "What will we tell the oldies?"

"Whatever you want," she yelled back.

I watched Danielle swinging farther and farther out on the rope before she dropped into the pool.

Dear God,
A word about Danielle.
She says I'm bossy, making decisions, but she's
reckless! If there was a war, they would use
her to do something very dangerous and she
would be brave and dead in no time.
And another thing — trees.
Trees are so helpless. They can't run and hide.
They just stand rooted to the spot.
That tree was probably growing there
before Captain Cook arrived in Australia!
After all those years it can be cut down so fast.
Please don't let anything happen to that
big tree.
Yours, Stressing about sisters
and trees.
Henni

In the Big Top that night, after Tibor had told us the story of how he once saw a bear in the wild, and after the mamas and the papas had blown kisses at us (because it was too dangerous to step through all the bodies and deliver kisses the usual way), they went back to the fire, and we were all snug in our sleeping bags, and friends again, which made us happy and crazy.

I remember Zev saying that some people drink their own

urine, and we wondered if we could bear to drink ours if we were dying of thirst. And Cass's story of the bow factory. You know all those bows on girls' undies? Well, Cass said there was this huge bow factory, with bow-making machines, and every day they sent truckloads of bows to the undies factory.

"Fiddle-up, fiddle-down, fiddleback," said Cass, testing the sound of the word. "Fiddleback. It's a funny one. I keep thinking about it."

"Might be a spider," said Frank. "You know how a redback has red on its back? Well, a fiddleback might have a fiddle on its back."

"I reckon it sounds like a nickname for a rugby player," said Cass. "Like the person who's stuck up the back and the ball never comes near them, so they just fiddle and diddle."

"A fiddle is a violin," I said. "Like a country violin."

"No, I think it's a lizard," said Frank. "A lizard that sort of fiddles with its back before it strikes."

"A swear word!" said Cass. "You know. Oh *fiddleback*! Like fiddle-dee-dee!"

"Well, they were sweary sort of men," said Danielle. "But that doesn't sound bad enough for them."

"I'm going to ask Dad tomorrow."

But we forgot about it.

17
Platypus

The good thing about being five kids is that you don't get stuck with the same sister all the time. Sometimes it was the "olds"— Zev and me—and the "youngs"—Cass, Dan, and Frank. Sometimes, Frank went with Rob or Donna for a while. Sometimes it was us girls. Plenty of choice. Sometimes, Zev pottered off by himself.

But I'm getting off the subject. At breakfast we asked about who owns trees.

"Whoever owns that land over there owns those trees," said Dad, waving at the tree-covered bank on the other side of the river. "They can do what they like with them."

"No, I think you have to get a permit to clear bush these days," said Rob.

"Well, nobody'd know what happens in this neck of the woods," said Dad.

"I think you'll find the forestry department has a fair idea," said Rob.

They had a slight argument. They weren't the only ones.

Danielle was being a pain again, too smart for her own boots or whatever the saying is. She had imitated me yawning, then she wanted me to fix her goggles for her.

"Do it yourself!" I snapped.

"What's wrong with you, scrawny-scrawn?"

"I am not scrawny!"

Donna called me. "Come on, Hen. Let's go for a little walk and leave these pesky insects behind. Grab your boots."

"Can we come, too?"

"No, buzz off."

First I showed Donna the remains of the old house where Cass found the little china foot. Donna walked quite easily. The going wasn't hard and we weren't in a hurry. We stopped for a rest.

"Don't let them get to you, Hen. You're growing up a bit, and feeling prickly. They're so used to you being easygoing." Donna leaned back against the trunk of a tree. "We've all been together in this spot for days now. I'm amazed at the way you kids get along so well."

Donna is lovely. Suddenly I just wanted to show her our valley, as a sort of present. I knew it would be special to her.

"Do you think you could walk a bit farther, Donna? There's somewhere I want to take you."

"We're fine, as long as we go slowly." Donna was calling herself "we" all the time now.

So I led her along the riverbank toward the creek. I was glad the others didn't see us go. (They must've been in the pool.)

They would have wanted to come, too. I knew they'd be cross with me for showing her the gully by myself, but I didn't care.

The walk seemed much steeper, and the bush thicker, probably because I was with Donna and kept thinking of Baby Watermelon. I held back branches so they wouldn't twang in her face, and gave her a hand up the steep bits.

"Phew!" said Donna. "Much farther?"

"Not far."

I laughed. "Usually we're saying, 'Much farther?' and you're saying, 'Not far.'"

Donna perched on a rock and surveyed the forest. "The vegetation's changing. This is really interesting."

Loud clear birdcalls rang through the gully. A thrush, a whipbird, a kookaburra, and a magpie.

We pushed on upward until we were in the dappled gloom, padding the soft forest floor beneath the plumes of ferns. Donna kept exclaiming, "Oh my goodness!" "Look at that!" or just "Ooh!" When we sat on the fallen log, she said in awe, "Rain forest here! Musk daisies and native hazel! These are blackwoods! Look at the size of that big one. Two hundred, maybe three hundred years old at least! What a precious wild place. Oh, Hen, isn't this wonderful?"

Donna was feasting on it. Her eyes—well, I wouldn't usually say this because it's corny and bookish, but it's true—her eyes were drinking it in. She breathed slowly and deeply, as if she was breathing in the forest and giving the place to her baby. We sat there side by side in the cool green, not talking, just watching, listening, breathing.

"I wonder why it's rain forest here?" Donna broke the silence. "There must be a source of water."

"It's really squelchy farther on." I showed her where Zev had almost got bogged.

"Maybe there's a soak in the side of the hill, oozing down the gully."

On the way back to camp, we rested beside the creek. Donna tapped my arm, silently pointing to a ripple in the clear water. It was a platypus! He was flipping along, busily wagging his head from side to side after food. His duck feet at the front were doing all the swimming. For easily five minutes, we watched him slipping around. Then suddenly he wasn't there.

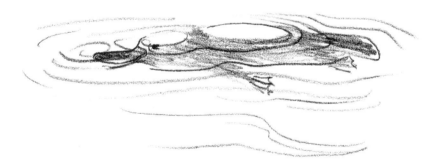

Everyone knows about the platypus, but to actually see one in the wild is rare, and I mean RARE! Back at camp, the others were green with envy.

"Hey, listen to this," said Dad, reading from *What Animal Is That?* "'When the first specimen . . . of platypus arrived at the British Museum, it was believed the extraordinary creature may have been a hoax.'"

Frank had his lips in the "what" position, but Rob beat him.

"A hoax is a trick to fool people."

Donna was in raptures about the gully. "This is how I would describe it," she said, putting on her botanical book voice. "A precious pocket of rain forest with an undisturbed stand of blackwood trees, some of them huge, being hundreds of years old. A freak of nature. A feast of botanical variety. A fortunate occurrence."

"This is how I would describe it," said Frank. "Cool!"

18
Looking for Old Jim

We were puddling in the clay at the edge of the pool, which is a good thing to do when you're thinking. Zev was modeling, I was drawing patterns, Frank was stirring up a muddy mixture, Danielle was winding a spider's web onto a stick, making a little sort of cotton bud, Cass was threading dead Christmas beetles to make a necklace, and we were talking about the gully.

I was right. The others were furious that I'd taken Donna there without them. Danielle, who had apologized to me for being rude that morning, took her apology back.

They couldn't see that it would have been different for Donna—less private—if all six of us had been there together. Actually, Zev understood. Anyway, I paid for my sins by sharing my precious last packet of Jaffas.

"I've got an awful feeling about those men," said Danielle.

"Me too!" said Cass.

"Who do you think owns that place?" said Zev.

"Owning things. Owning owning moaning groaning!" said Danielle. "What a fuss there is about owning things."

It seemed really odd to be talking about somebody *owning*

the gully. As if it *could* be owned. It sounded so wrong. Like, can someone *own* a rainbow? Can someone *own* a waterfall?

"Old Jim would know about all this," said Zev.

"It might be his."

"Maybe we should ask him," said Cass.

"Yes! Let's find his house."

"I don't think we should *all* go," I said.

But nobody wanted to stay behind. Surprise, surprise.

We took the food to the Talk Rocks and threw it over to Heap.

"We're like zookeepers," said Danielle out of the corner of her mouth, and we all felt a bit uncomfortable.

"Definitely not today!" we said firmly about seeing Donna.

Heap didn't seem to mind. "Tomorrow, then."

"Do you know about an old guy who lives around here somewhere?" asked Cass.

"Up there," said Heap, waving his arm at the top of the ridge. "I seen him."

"On your side of the river?"

"Yeah, but right around the valley."

"Very far?"

"A fair way. Uphill. At the top." He pointed at a peak.

"Thanks."

"See ya tomorrow."

"See ya."

"Ready for the instructions?" whispered Cass as we approached the parents and Mr. Nic, who were sitting around laughing like mad about something. (It must have been rude, or about us, because they stopped when we got close.)

"We're going exploring," Danielle announced.

Yep! We got all the instructions.

"Wear thick socks and put on your shoes."

"Carry a stick."

"Take some water and some fruit."

"Make a lot of noise to scare the snakes."

Tibor laughed. "No need to worry about that one!"

"Stick together and remember where you are."

"Be back no later than six, okay?"

Sue put down her book and gave us a funny look over her glasses. "What are you lot up to, eh? Until a day or so ago, you were quite happy to flop around in the river. Now you're off all over the place. "

"We're kidnapping the president!" said Danielle.

"There's just so much to explore," said Zev, sounding suspiciously like one of the Brady Bunch.

Being tall is a responsibility. When I'm walking down the street, people collecting for charity always shake their cans under my nose because I stand out like a lighthouse. Adults always ask *me* the questions. So, although I didn't want the job, and Zev is older than me by a month and a day, I ended up being Expedition Leader—as always.

I was worried firstly about getting lost, and secondly about *all* of us going to see Old Jim. Can you imagine visiting a bush hermit with Danielle and Cass waving their feet in the air all the time, Zev grinning like a strange-haired Cheshire cat, Frank going his own sweet way, *and* a mad sausage dog who might drop a stinking hoof in your lap? Not the ideal companions for delicate diplomatic detective work. People who choose to live out in the bush by themselves don't want five city kids dropping in. He probably only saw kids when he went to town once a month. And five kids is quite a lot of kids—for a hermit.

"We're going to the ford. Can you keep Briquette?" I called in my most casual, natural voice.

We did cross the ford, and then went back along the track until we found what looked like a path. We bashed our way along it for a while, climbing as we went. Looking down through the trees, we could just see our camp. The three smaller tents looked like bright moths settled on the ground. All our man-made junk was so colorful in the dull bush.

"This doesn't feel like a path anymore," said Cass.

"You've gone the wrong way!" yelled Frank, who was getting left behind.

"Good one, Frank."

Being the youngest, Frank's closer to the ground than the rest of us.

So we crashed on up his path, away from the campsite.

After a long haul up and up the hill, Zev at the front suddenly yelled, "Hey! A dog! And I think it's Old Jim's!"

"Here, boy! Here, boy!"

The dog stood growling ever so quietly. Then his tail gave a one-millimeter wag, and with a toss of his head, as if to say, "Why not!," he loped toward us, sort of sideways, wagging his tail, which wagged the whole of his rump.

"I think he's our friend now," said Frank as the dog nearly knocked him flying.

"Okay, home, boy, home. Take us to your place."

But the dog grinned at us, as if to say, "What now? More pats?"

"Be boring, then he'll go home," said Cass.

So we froze. The dog couldn't understand what had happened to his new friends. He licked and jumped and barked. Finally he gave up and trotted off. Not much farther on, the rough track met a definite track.

Ten minutes later, we walked into a clearing on the ridge,

and there was Old Jim's hut with a bird's-eye view down the river valley. No doubt about it, because sitting on the veranda like this was Old Jim.

He looked at us in a stony way, as if we were Martians.

My heart sank.

19
Five Kids and a Hermit

So there's this dodgy old man and us five kids. We stood, feeling awkward, with him looking down on us like a judge.

"What do y' want?"

I thought how it would ruin the whole trip if he didn't like us, or was sorry he ever told Miriam about the spot on the river.

Frank said, "What sort of a dog is your dog?"

"A bitza."

"What's a bitza?"

"Bitza this, bitza that. Cattle dog. Kelpie."

"What's his name?"

"Some people want to know what y' had for breakfast," said Old Jim, ignoring the question and staring over our heads.

"What *did* you have for breakfast?" asked Frank.

My heart sank further.

"What do y' want?" asked the old man again.

"Shhhh!" I hissed at Frank; then I cleared my throat and put on my responsible-young-lady voice. "We've come to ask what a fiddleback is."

"What's that?" said Old Jim.

"A fiddleback."

I kept thinking, "He likes books, he loved Donna and Miriam's mum." (Come on, Old Jim. Crack one of those walnut smiles.)

"I don't know what y' mean by *a* fiddleback."

None of us knew what to say next.

"Are y' talkin' about fiddleback as an adjective, rather than a noun?"

"Yes," I said, eager for anything.

"Fiddleback's a pattern in timber, like ripples in the grain. Beautiful enough for the back of a violin."

"Have you seen a violin with a fiddleback back?" asked Cass.

"My oath," said Old Jim. "Heard it, too."

He was thawing. (Come on, Old Jim, give us a smile.)

"How can you tell if a tree has fiddleback wood?" asked Zev.

"If y' cut a nick, y'll see it in the grain."

I caught Zev's eye.

"What makes it fiddleback?" asked Cass.

"I dunno. There's various theories." He was definitely thawing. "Some say it's in the DNA of the tree."

It was amazing to hear this old bush voice talking about stuff like DNA. Danielle and Frank were patting the dog, but Cass, Zev, and I were listening closely. We kept shouting our questions to him up on the veranda.

"I reckon it's caused by compression. For example, if the prevailin' wind's from the west"—and he stood up with his arms out as branches and bent over sideways, as if he was a tree with the prevailing wind from the west—"you'll get y' fiddleback on the east"—and he pointed to the wrinkles in his vest on that side of his body. "But it can run all through a tree."

"Does it only happen in one sort of tree?"

"Nah, y' get y' fiddleback in all sorts of trees. What's all this business about fiddleback?"

(Give us a walnut smile, please, Old Jim.)

So I started to tell him Danielle's story of the men who came to our camp. He leaned forward, listening so hard I thought he might topple down the steps.

"For goodness' sake, come closer," he said. "I'm not gunna bite ya."

Then, I don't know why, maybe because it was so exciting and it was her story and she wasn't telling it, but Danielle suddenly did a cartwheel.

"Does she always do that?" Old Jim cracked a smile.

"Yes!" We all sort of breathed out at last.

"Righty-o, now where did these chaps cut this tree?" he said cheerfully.

Zev explained how we followed their tracks to the gully. His smile faded and he straightened up.

"Yeah, I know that gully," he said. "I was hopin' y' wouldn't find it. Go on."

Zev told him about the cut in the big tree.

"By crikey! The big blackwood, eh?" He rubbed his stomach as if he had a guts-ache. The walnut smile was gone. He started thinking aloud.

"Anyone interested in somethin' as big as that'd have to be from the mill."

"I beg your pardon?" I said.

"See, this place is crawlin' with Mattocks. The mill's a funny sort of turn-out. Owned by a Melbourne woman. Her husband died. You can bet she doesn't know about all this. Mattock runs the mill, and Mattock's as mad as a meat ax."

"Do you think they cut the tree to see if it was fiddleback?" said Zev.

"Yeah. They'd be checkin' it. He'd have his eye on something that size." Old Jim shook his head slowly. "Money-grubbin' mongrel. I don't think Mattock's ever seen a beautiful tree in his life."

"Who owns the gully?" I asked gingerly. I knew this was a prickly question because anything to do with property seems to make people touchy.

Old Jim looked preoccupied for a moment, then he sighed and said, "Someone up Queensland way."

20
Old Jim's Hut

On one side of Old Jim's hut, there were walnut and apple trees, and the same sort of plum tree as near our camp. There was a garden, with a high chicken-wire fence, growing inedible leafy things like silver beet and rhubarb. Old Jim saw me looking at them. "Y' get a bit tired of corned beef and spuds," he said. "Used to have a little Jersey cow. A terrific milker, but she was too much trouble. Had chickens, too. Had to lock 'em up at night. Mr. Reynard finally got 'em."

"Who?"

"The fox."

There was a yard with a trough for

horses and cows. The water was pumped up by a funny sort of pump that kept going boink . . . boink . . . boink. . . .

"Still got nine head a' cattle," said Old Jim.

A dilapidated truck with the license plate GOB 020 rusted away in an old shed, with mining equipment and fishing rods leaning against the walls. Beside it was a hollow log with hide stretched over one end—the dog's kennel. The dog ate and drank from dinted hubcaps.

"Our dog found an old hoof," said Frank.

"Y' get unbranded cattle pokin' around in the bush. It'd be one of them that's come to grief," said Old Jim.

At the woodshed, beside the chopping block and the ax, there was a curious wheel thing set up with leather straps connected to some gears and a saw bench. I couldn't

understand it, but Zev did, and he laughed. "Does it work?"

"My oath!" said Old Jim. Then he gave a deafening whistle through his old teeth, and his dog came bounding around the corner of the hut. "Hop up!" he said. The dog leaped eagerly into the wheel and started running and running, making it turn, just like a mouse on one of those exercise wheels. There was a bit of carpet inside the wheel to make it easier for the dog's feet. Both the dog and Old Jim were really pleased when we laughed and clapped.

"Saws wood for me," said Old Jim proudly. "Got it out of a book! Hop down. Hop down," he said to the dog, who didn't want to stop. But when he took the lid off a nearby container and reached in, the dog leaped out of the wheel. "Got to give 'im 'is pay. Dog nuts. He loves 'em."

The hut was made of corrugated iron and split boards, like trees cut in half. It had two windows with glass, and a plain wooden door, and all around were old-fashioned tools, shovels, a pick, buckets, a watering can, a wheelbarrow, and saws, and bits of wire, and a pan for finding gold.

"Now, would y' like to see a nice bit of fiddleback?"

Of course we would.

"Well, y'd better come inside, then." Old Jim had become very sociable.

We'd never been in such a place. Imagine a room that has never been cleaned, ever. Things just sat where they were put ten, maybe twenty years ago. Everything was covered with spider's webs and dust, but it didn't really feel dirty except for the grime around the basin, the table, and a stove, made of black iron and set into a big fireplace.

"This stove was packed in," said Old Jim.

"What was it packed in?" asked Danielle.

He looked at her as if she was a baby. "Brought in by packhorse."

All his possessions looked old-fashioned, but there were surprises.

"Excuse me," said Zev. "Is this a radio?"

"Certainly is," said Old Jim. "Bought it by mail. Fairly recent invention. They use 'em in Africa, y' know. Y' wind 'em up. Yeah, go on, wind 'er up."

He rummaged in some shelves made from packing cases, then found a handmade box and wiped the top of it with his shirt.

"There. That's a nice piece of fiddleback."

The wood on the lid of the box was wonderful. It looked like wavy golden hair. It was so 3-D we all reached out to feel it, but it was flat.

"Trick wood!" said Cass.

There was just so much to look at in this dark cave of a hut: an oilskin coat, heavy boots, a gun, candles, mysterious ancient jars, tins and bottles, a big bag of onions, a picture of Niagara Falls, a bucket of sticks, batteries in a row, and a kangaroo skin on the floor by his lumpy-looking bed. One corner had rough wooden shelves which held all his books.

"Have you been here a long time?" asked Frank. Danielle gave him a derr-dumb-question look.

"Been up here all m' life, trappin' dingoes, grubbin' briers, doin' a bit of fencin.' Don't go down to town much. Too many gates to open, for a start. Only go down when I need fresh tucker. Y' can't hear yourself think down there."

"Here, have one of these." He unscrewed the top of a jar and offered it around. You had to hold the jar tight because all the barley sugar was stuck together in a fifty-year-old lump.

He tapped Frank on the shoulder. "Son, the dog's name's Timber."

21
The Dulugar

"Who's that kid?" Old Jim asked suddenly.

"Which kid?" said Zev.

"That wombat of a human who's sleepin' out around here."

We laughed because it was the best description of Heap.

We told him Heap's miserable story.

"Well, he seems to be gettin' on all right. He was up the top of the ridge the other day, talkin' to the forestry blokes. When I first saw him, I thought he was a Dulugar."

"Pardon?" said Zev.

"Well . . . I s'pose you'd best describe a Dulugar as . . . I dunno . . . a sort of spirit."

"A ghost?" squeaked Frank.

"Not exactly. If Old Percy was here, he'd tell ya."

"Who's Old Percy?" said Cass.

Old Jim had the habit of thinking that you knew who he was talking about, and not joining up his ideas, so we had to keep guessing and asking him questions. But we didn't know what to call him. Old Jim? Jim? Mister? They might be rude, so we didn't call him anything.

"Old Percy Longleg. Knew these hills like the back of his

hand. Had a word for everything, not in English, of course. Learned a lot from Old Percy. Often think of all the experience an' knowledge of the bush we lost when Old Perce died."

"Why didn't he speak English?" asked Cass.

"He was an Aborigine. He spoke some."

"Cool!" said Cass.

"What's a Dulugar like?" said Zev, tuning Old Jim back onto the subject, like a radio.

"Well, according to Old Percy, they're hairy all over, if I remember rightly . . ." He patted his pockets, looking for something, and his eyes roved around the room. "With long arms, no neck to speak of. And they're strong. Fearful things, he reckoned." He kept talking, but his eyes were searching for something the whole time. "I could tell you better about the Dulugar if I could find m' pipe. Can y' see it anywhere?"

We hunted.

"They reckon the Dulugar knows when there's women around. He likes 'em."

"Here it is!" Frank found the pipe behind a tin of flour.

"Good man."

Old Jim settled himself in his chair and knocked the ash from his pipe into a little drawer sticking out from the stove. Then he dug around in the pipe bowl with a nail and tapped out more ash.

"Gotta be extra careful about fire this time of ycar."

Then he fished an ancient leather wallet from his possum vest pocket and took a pinch of something. It smelled nice.

"What's that stuff?" asked Danielle.

"Pipe tobacco," said Old Jim. "You shouldn't smoke. It's bad for ya."

His yellowed fingers pushed the shreds of tobacco into the bowl of his pipe till it was packed, then he started patting his pockets again. "Anyone seen m' matches?"

Cass tossed him the box. He struck a match, held it over the tobacco, and sucked on the pipe. The flame was sucked down onto the tobacco. He kept giving the pipe quick sucks until he was happy that the little fire was alight. It didn't flame up, just smoldered. Then he leaned back, ready to tell the story.

"We used to get the Melbourne Women's Walking Club up here," he continued. "Mind you, this is goin' back a bit. I was their guide for a time. Well, Old Percy was a bit of a character, and he'd hop around an' get concerned an' tell me not to let 'em go off by themselves because of the Dulugar. But these women, y' know, they were a pretty strong-minded mob. Never took much notice. They'd go off alone to water the bushes, and so forth."

He sucked on his pipe, which sat neatly in the corner of his mouth, between a gap in his teeth, so he could still talk with the rest of his mouth.

"Then one day this woman comes back all shaken up and

sayin' this hairy thing grabbed 'er and she reckons she just managed to fight it off. Well, they made light of it, joked about how she was partial to a little nip, and caught in the ferns and that, but I'll tell you somethin', they never came back up here again."

"Have you ever seen a Dulugar?" asked Cass.

"No," said Old Jim, "but I thought I had when I saw your friend."

Then there was silence.

"You never know, in this country . . ."

"Can I have a go of your pipe?" said Frank.

Old Jim looked at him. "It's not a peace pipe, y' know."

"Just a little go?" said Frank.

So we all had a puff of the pipe while Old Jim laughed at our coughing, till he started coughing himself.

"Now, how about a cuppa tea?"

While he was making the tea, I had a good look at his books. They were about every subject you could imagine: water divining, insects, buffalo hunting, Shakespeare, rocks, God— absolutely everything. There were a few novels and four small leather-bound books, very worn. I opened one very carefully. It was a notebook filled with fine pencil handwriting, quotations on life, books he'd read, poetry written by Old Jim, how many dingoes he trapped, how many briers he grubbed out, fish caught, how much he got paid, how much he spent, birds' nests, sightings of animals . . . His whole life was in these little books. Suddenly I felt terrible. I was trespassing. I slipped them back and stole away from the bookshelves.

Old Jim poured the tea from an awful brown pot—all chipped and stained, that had once been white with roses—into rusty enamel mugs that looked like they hadn't been washed for fifty years.

"Do you think it's okay to drink?" whispered Frank.

I nodded, hoping I was right.

"Have you ever seen a tree struck by lightning?" asked Zev.

"Now, there's a question!" said Old Jim. We could tell it had a long answer.

"Y' get different trees either side of the ridge. See, y' north is dryer and y' south is wetter. Doesn't get the sun, see. Different vegetation, different species. Mattock cut tracks wherever he wanted."

I couldn't see how this had anything to do with lightning. He was still thinking about the fiddleback blackwood. "He'd winch it up from a 'dozer . . . make a fine mess of it."

Danielle snuck outside and poured her tea on a bush.

"What was it y' wanted to know, son?"

"Lightning," Zev prompted.

"Right. See that patch of dead wood up there?" He pointed through the window to a group of bare branches in the timber up on the ridge. "Storms roll up to the high country. Those trees are the first things they hit. All got lightnin' strikes down the side of 'em. Top's dead, and a strip of wood down one side. But it doesn't necessarily kill 'em. Strips the bark off as it goes down, earthin' through the sap. Lightnin' can start a fire, specially if it strikes fluffy messmate bark—all frayed and quick to light."

Suddenly, Zev pulled a face at his watch. "Jolts volts! We're going to be late!"

"Well, y'd better go, then," said the old man sadly. "It's a funny feelin', ya know, to see young faces up here after bein' by y'self for so long."

"I thought you'd be mad at us all for coming," I said to Old Jim. "I was really worried."

"Trouble with you, Hen, is you think too much," said Danielle.

Old Jim patted my shoulder. "That's my problem, too!"

"Now, seein' as you're so interested, I'll tell y' one more thing before y' go. An' I don't go tellin' everybody this. There are lyrebirds in that blackwood gully. Y' can *hear* 'em all right, loud and clear, but if you want to *see* 'im puttin' on his act, you'll have to sneak up on 'im. Not like y' came bargin' up here. I heard y' comin' a mile away."

He shook all our hands.

"That *was* a peace pipe," said Cass.

Old Jim climbed back onto his veranda. "Like m' beautiful scenery?" He waved at the view.

"Cool!"

"See y' again sometime. Tell the old chap to call in for a cuppa tea and a yarn. Tell 'im to bring y' newspapers when you've finished with 'em. Don't mind how old they are."

It was downhill all the way back. We flew like the wind and got scratched and prickled and ripped. We were very late, but the grown-ups had been fishing and Mr. Nic had actually caught a trout, so they hadn't noticed the time.

We collapsed on the ground, exhausted.

"We're boiling and we're busting and we're starving!"

"Where did you go?"

"We visited Old Jim."

"Well, did you now! How is he? We could have come, too."

"Mr. Nic, he wants you to visit him and take the newspapers."

"You should see his place. It's all homemade," said Frank.

"And we tried his pipe, and he gave us a revolting cup of tea," said Cass.

"And he told us about the Dulugar, a hairy spirit that comes down from the mountains and grabs ladies," said Danielle.

The adults listened to every word about our expedition to the hut.

"You have to take Old Jim's stories with a grain of salt," said Donna.

"Talking of salt, besides trout, what'll we have for dinner?" said Sue, looking at the kitchen boxes. "Wish we could order pizza."

"I'll cook," said Mr. Nic. "What do you want me to cook? This is what I can cook on a fire: charcoal chicken, charcoal chops, charcoal sausages, charcoal spud, charcoal tomato, anything you like—charcoal."

That evening was chilly. It was hard to believe after the hot day. We sat around the fire.

"Donna, tell us about Old Jim," said Cass.

So she did. It was such a sad story. Donna and Miriam's mum was called Dorothy. Jim (who wasn't old then) met Dorothy at a country dance. Dorothy was about twenty. Now, they loved each other, the story goes, and they went out together a lot. But then Jim went away somewhere, and when he returned, Dorothy had married Donna's father because she thought Jim wasn't coming back. He never wrote to her or anybody.

And here's the saddest part. After her husband died, Dorothy lived on her own for a long time. When she finally died, Old Jim heard about her funeral and traveled all the way to Bairnsdale to go to it. And when he heard she'd been living alone for the last fifteen years, he cried. That's what they say.

It was strange hearing about this and knowing Donna and Miriam. I made a note right then: if I ever love somebody I'm going to keep track of them, even if they are married, whatever happens. Especially these days. Lots of marriages don't last long.

You never think of old people having boyfriends or girlfriends or feeling that fiery passion sort of love. You just think of the old-slipper kind of love, which is nice, too, I suppose.

22
Mad as Meat Axes

The sun was strong. With his little magnifying glass, Zev could burn his name in paper in a second. He was always experimenting with his walkie-talkie or something from his inventions bag.

The first event of the morning was finding that Briquette's blanket had maggots. Obviously, it was ripe for it. Briquette goggled at us as we washed her blanket in the river downstream and bashed it on the rocks. She fussed around barking, "What are you doing to my blanket?"

Donna took herself off for a swim.

"I must say it's wonderful to see Donna so relaxd," said Tibor.

"She's floating . . . literally!" We could just see her in the pool over by the Government Rocks. She was dabbling around, keeping to her own time, going for little naps.

"She said she had a couple of Braxton Hicks," said Rob with his nose in *What Baby Is That?*

"What's Braxton Hicks?" said Tibor. "Didn't he invent the steam train or something?"

"Here it is," said Rob. "Uh-oh! It's a sort of contraction."

"What sort of contraption?" said Frank. (Sometimes he does that just to be cute!)

"Contraction. When the muscles in the womb go hard. It doesn't hurt at first, just hardens up somehow. The book says, 'This may happen some time before the baby is born.' I wonder how long before?" said Rob. "I'd better talk to Donna."

Dad was restless and itchy to do something, so even though it was hot, he persuaded the other adults, even Mr. Nic, to cross the river and climb to the top of the ridge.

"I'm going to have a lovely little snooze!" said Donna as soon as the others were gone, as if it was a deliciously naughty thing to do.

"What if they come across Heap's camp?" said Cass.

"I'd like to see it," said Frank, paddling his toes in the water.

That morning, when Heap threw back the ice cream container, he'd put the head of a marsupial mouse in it, wrapped in bark. It became one of our treasures.

We played Pop Bango, then we'd just started inventing this game called Rockhoppers, when Cass yelled out, "A car!"

Squealing and screeching, we dived for clothes. (We had some on, but not everywhere.) Then we looked out from behind the kitchen stuff to see who it was.

Ladies and jelly beans, grown-ups and grown-downs, fasten your seat belts and put your tray tables in an upright position, because this is where the turbulence begins!

A four-wheel drive stopped not far from the tents. Both doors opened at the same time and two men climbed out and looked around. One was older, bigger, and rougher, with a huge beer gut. The younger one had to be a chip off the old block because he had exactly the same-shaped nose. He was about twenty, I guess. They looked around, then got out fishing rods and a bucket.

They walked over to us. "G'day. Your parents around?"

Well, at this point Donna bleared out of the tent. She'd been asleep.

"G'day. Stan Mattock's the name. This is Darren."

Danielle cleared her throat for about thirty seconds, so only an idiot wouldn't get the message.

"Hot enough for ya?"

"Yes. Pretty warm," said Donna, pushing back her hair, not pleased she'd been woken up from her snooze to talk about the weather.

"Great little spot y' got here."

"Yes, isn't it."

"Where y' from?"

"Melbourne."

"Oh yeah. We often come down here to try our luck." He gave a little wave of the fishing rod.

I caught Zev's eye and his look said, "*Liar!*"

"How'd y' find out about this place?"

"Friend told us." If Donna likes someone, she's normally putting on the kettle for a cup of tea by now. But she wasn't giving an inch. We all knew this chitchat was leading to something. Mattock put his hand on his hip.

"Now, you know this land is private property?"

"Do *you* own this land?" asked Donna. That foiled him a bit. I think he wanted us to think he did.

"Well, actually, I've got a message from the owner." He cleared his throat. "He'd like you out of here by Friday."

We knew it was a lie. Old Jim had said the owner was dead, and if there was a new owner, he wasn't worried about it.

Now, Donna has been listening to lies for years as part of her work. She's good at telling where a person's coming from.

"Could you give us the details of the owner, and we'll have a word with them?"

"No. Can't do that. I've got strict instructions he'd like you out of here."

Then, like a bolt of lightning, Danielle—the human lie detector—came out with, "You want to cut down that fiddleback blackwood tree, don't you!"

Mattock was completely taken by surprise. He rubbed his big nose on his arm and scratched his head. As for Darren, he turned bright red and his eyebrows shot up so high they disappeared into his hair.

"What I do is my business," blustered Mattock. Then, "What the hell are you talking about?"

It was a dead giveaway!

"I knew it!" said Danielle.

Donna was horrified. "Are you talking about the blackwood trees in the gully? *Surely* not!"

The big man didn't know what to do, and he didn't have the wits to cover up. So there was Mattock, with his big beer gut out the front of him, and there was Donna, with Baby Watermelon.

Donna looked him straight in the eye. "Is this true?"

"Look, lady, if you were back in your little home, you wouldn't know a thing about this place. You wouldn't know there were trees here, and if we cut 'em down, you wouldn't care."

"But we *do* know about them," I said. "That's the difference."

"I'm not talking to you, miss!" he barked. "You lot think trees are something magical. Well, I'll tell you what they are. They're trees. And you know something? They grow up out of the ground. Did you ever hear that? That new trees can grow up out of the ground?"

"But that place is rare!"

"Oh God. Bloody tree-weepers!" Mattock was getting steamed up.

"What about the animals and birds?" said Cass. "You chop down their habitat—"

"Habitat! Habitat! Why don't you go back to your precious habitat in the city and mind your own bloody business?"

"This *is* my business," said Donna.

"Since when?"

"Since I saw it. That place is rare. If you knew anything about the bush, you'd know that little gully's a freak of nature. Blackwoodus somethingorotheris in this area."

I think it was Donna saying the proper Latin name for the trees that sent him right off.

"Smart-fart know-all city people! You blow in here and think you own the bloody place."

I hated the way he talked down to Donna and us kids as if we knew nothing.

"Look, lady, there's plenty of bush for all your precious creepies and crawlies."

"But if you keep chopping down old forest, there won't be."

"Now, don't give me that 'old forest' line. Do you know how

much old forest there is? Plenty, okay? Take my word for it."

"I wouldn't take your word for anything," said Donna, tight-lipped.

"Simmer down, little lady," he smirked. "In your state, you shouldn't be getting yourself all worked up. Look, you pack up and go home and tell everybody you had a nice vacation in the bush and just forget all about it."

"That gully is unique!"

"Oh, your type, you *love* that word 'unique.' Look, every bloody thing's unique!"

"Mr. Mattock, that little pocket of rain forest is rare. We don't know what's living there. Nobody's studied it. Once you've cut down those trees, the gully is gone. They're hundreds of years old."

"About four hun—" Darren chipped in.

"*Shut up!*" his father snapped.

"You couldn't get them out without ripping the gully to shreds."

"You just chop down trees because you can't do anything else," said Danielle. "And you can't change your ideas."

I thought he was going to explode.

"Danielle, be *quiet*! That's *enough*!" said Donna.

He glared at Danielle, then at Donna, as if to say, "Do something about her!"

"If you were my kid—"

"I'd suicide!"

We could see he was itching to hit her, but instead he turned and swung a kick at Briquette. He caught her in the ribs, and she raced away yelping.

"Get your bloody dog out of my way."

"If she's injured, you'll answer for it," shouted Donna, furious.

"Thickness!" Danielle yelled after him.

"*Danielle. Be quiet!*" Donna snapped.

"I'm warnin' ya!" he flung back at us. He didn't even pretend about the fishing.

Mattock hurled his rod into the back of the vehicle and flung the bucket after it, slamming the car door. Darren followed, a pathetic imitation of his father.

"Don't touch that gully!" yelled Donna.

"I'll do what I bloody well like!" yelled Mattock over the engine noise.

"Don't!"

"Who's going to stop me?"

"Us."

"You and whose army?" He shook his fist at Danielle and revved the engine till it roared. "You'll be out of here, you'll see." He drove off in a fury.

"With any luck he'll have an accident!" said Danielle.

Cass tossed her hair. "Who cares a pumpkin's knob about him!"

"I need to sit down," said Donna. "That timber miller is the most absolute form of monster."

"How was the son, Darren?" said Zev. "Boy, that guy's a loser. How'd you be with a dad like *that*!"

"I hate the way he toadied to his father."

"We are guarding the gully," I said.

"Yes, we are," said Danielle.

I felt so sorry for Briquette, I found something to comfort her. It was wrapped in three plastic bags in a tin in the boot of the car where Rob had put it. The hoof.

When the other adults arrived home, there was a serious top-level debriefing. First we told them about the men Danielle had heard (she still wouldn't tell us her hiding spot), then about our visit to the gully, then everything Old Jim told us, then—in vivid detail—our encounter with Mad Mattock. It was scary, but actually we sort of enjoyed it. The adults were concerned because Donna was stressed to the max.

"I think you should have a rest," said Rob.

"We're fine," said Donna.

"Sounds like he can't see the trees for the wood."

"Tomorrow we'll go back to Old Jim's and find out what he knows about all this."

After dinner Briquette trotted into the light with a big silly grin—and her hoof.

"How did she get that?"

I confessed. Rob took the hoof, walked downstream, and flung it into a deep rocky pool.

"There, that'll give the fish something to think about."

Briquette ran up and down the bank, whining for her hoof.

In the Big Top that night, it took us ages to get to sleep. We made up stories about Mad Mattock, and Old Mad Ma Mattock, and the mini Mad Mattocks, and all the Mad Mattock Mob, and their fat pet Dog, and their dumpy daughters, Phleg, Prag, and quick Insta, and the son, Auto, who pathetically copied his father. . . .

Dear God,
    About Danielle again.
Her anger is scary. She gets a charge of power when she's mad. It usually works out... but she's clumsy...
    Now that we're guarding the gully please watch her. At least she's got a good hiding spot.

    yours,
      Sleepless in The Bush.

PS And Briquette, too!

23
Bombast

"Bombast," said Dad next morning at breakfast. "Bluster. It won't come to anything. Mattock tried to call your bluff, but you stood up to him. He'll give up. End of event."

"No way," we said. "You don't understand. He's a ratbag. He's brutal. He's dangerous. Honestly!" Donna backed us up.

But Dad couldn't believe it. The other adults listened and believed us, but not Dad.

Until then, camping had been no particular hour of the day, no particular day of the week, no month, no year—just a glorious bush no-time. But ever since we'd arrived, Dad had been craving a newspaper. By now, he was desperate. He'd even started to read the greasy blackened six-months-old news that was wrapped around the jaffle irons. When he finished his cup of coffee, he stood up and stretched.

"Wait," said Mum. "I know what you're going to say!"

"What?" said Dad.

"Think I'll drive into town."

Everyone laughed, including Dad.

"Well, you're all so steamed up about this Mad Mattock business, we'd better find out about this place. Might get a paper while I'm there," he threw in casually, and everybody laughed because it was like someone dying of thirst saying, "Might just have a drink."

"Want anything from the shops?"

"Cold beer!"

"In cans."

"Ice."

"Anything you can lay your hands on that's *fresh*."

So Dad and Mr. Nic took a whole lot of stuff out of our car and turned it back from a shed to a car, and put in the two big coolers, and found their wallets, and listened to the instructions about shopping lists, and then—with Zev and Danielle—they bumped out of the clearing and off to town.

"Go carefully," called Tibor, "the place might be swarming with Mattocks, all mad as meat axes."

As soon as they were gone, I took the food to Heap. I was glad Danielle wasn't there, although she'd stopped making a scene. Heap looked as wild as ever, but there was something about him—he'd lost weight. If he was living on what we gave him, no wonder. But also he looked straighter, fitter.

Rob tied on his boots. "Take me to Old Jim's," he said, "and we'll see what he knows about all this."

So Cass and I stuffed some dried apricots in our pockets, put a bottle of water in the daypack, and set off with ancient newspapers and December's *Time* magazine as a present for

Old Jim. Frank was happy to stay with Donna, Sue, and Mum, who were going up to the gully. And Tibor was making something.

It was a good walk. Cass and I talked about school, and Rob spotted a beehive in a hollow tree. But Timber didn't come to meet us. We got to the hut quite easily. There was no sign of the old man. We called out, "Hello? Anyone home?" but there was no answer. The old truck was gone from the shed.

"I didn't think that bomb would go!" said Cass.

Timber was there, tied up and very happy to see us. He barked and jumped and wagged his tail, but we didn't think we should let him off the chain.

"In some places, they'd sell you tickets for this," said Rob, "and call it a living museum. All this gear from the last century. But look up on the roof! He's got a solar panel! Wonder what that's for?"

Rob was fascinated by the wheel for Timber.

"A dog treadmill! I've never seen anything like it."

"You should see inside," said Cass. "It's unbelievable."

"What do you think?" said Rob. "Okay to have a quick peep?"

Slowly he pushed open the door. We gasped. There was stuff everywhere. The place had been ransacked!

"Two days ago, it was like nothing had been moved for fifty years," gabbled Cass. "Now you'd think a hurricane had hit."

"Don't touch anything," said Rob.

We didn't go any farther into the hut, just stood by the door and looked.

Then I noticed something. "It's been done carefully. Look. Nothing's smashed or tipped upside down. They've just been moved. See, the books are in piles. It looks awful because of the spiders and the dust, but I don't think it was a robber. I think Old Jim did it."

"Well," said Rob. "I don't know if it's our business or not."

We stepped outside, and he pulled the door closed behind him.

"I don't know what to think."

"What if Mad Mattock . . . What happened, Timber?"

The dog didn't seem worried, so we left the newpapers on the veranda chair and went back to camp, talking the whole way about Old Jim and what might have happened at the hut.

The shopping party returned, gleeful and triumphant, early in the afternoon.

"Talk about lucky!" shrieked Danielle, exploding out of the car. "We went to the county office and it was absolutely shut till January the twenty-first, but I knocked a loud hard knock anyway, and just when we were getting back into the car, a man opened the door—"

"He had come in to finish some report," said Zev.

"—with big ears," said Danielle. "And he was very bored and he talked and talked and talked and *talked*. And when Dad said we wanted to know about the place where we were camping, he found this map and that map, and maps and maps and maps of *everything*, and photocopied them *all* for us."

"This place has a name!" said Zev. "We're staying at Bacon Flat."

"That's because the drovers used to have their breakfast here. You can't get to the gully except by going through Bacon Flat and up the river."

"And then—" said Dad, but he didn't get a chance.

"We found out about Mad Mattock!" Danielle burst in. "He's the timber mill manager and everyone *hates* him. He cut a track on the wrong side of the ridge and it's caused erosion. Remember what Old Jim said? And the owner of the mill lives in Melbourne and she never comes down to the mill, so she doesn't know what he's really like. And now Dad finally believes that he's someone to watch out for."

We all needed food after that, so we had a feast of a lunch, with fresh cherries, peaches, cheese, and bread.

"What are we going to do about Mr. Mattock?" I asked.

While we munched, we chewed over the problem, then Dad, Mum, Sue, and Tibor all settled down to read different bits of the newspaper, which was absolutely maddening.

God,
How can they read newspapers
at a time like this?
<u>Newspapers</u> of all things!
What about Mattock -
isn't he news?
At least Dad believes he's
a maniac now. I suppose I
should be relieved.

Yours,
extremely cheesed off!
Henni

PS When we put our newspapers
out at home in Stella Street
are they really recycled?

124

We didn't know what to do. Donna slipped in for a swim. When she came out, she noticed us looking at her swollen body—without really looking, if you know what I mean.

"Do you want to inspect Baby Watermelon?" She was totally unembarrassed, and took off the towel.

"Oh, Donna, your belly button's sticking out!"

"Well, there's no room left inside. Feel!"

Her skin was stretched as tight as a drum. Then a bump moved.

"Wow, did you see that?" said Cass.

"Donna, you're possessed! You've got something living inside you!"

She laughed. "Don't I know it!"

The bump moved again. We stared.

"I think that's a foot," she said, feeling the hard little knob with her hand. "What do you think?"

We all had a feel and agreed it was a heel.

"If you put your ear to my belly, you can hear the heartbeat." We all had a listen.

"It's very quick," said Cass. "Sounds like a little donkey trotting along."

"Hello, Baby Watermelon!" said Frank. "Hurry up so I can play with you."

"It's pretty tight in here," said Donna. "That's why I keep going to the toilet. I'm pregnant up to my eyes! No room left."

"When's it going to happen?" asked Cass.

"Who knows?"

Donna wrapped the towel around her big self and slipped on her thongs. "I'm going to have a nap now," she said, "and when I wake up, I want you to come with me, Henni and Zev, to carry my plant books and write for me. We're going to the gully. We're going to start work."

At least somebody was going to do something!

24
A Visit from Joe Blakes

We all felt twitchy, what with Mad Mattock and the fiddleback and Old Jim, but we couldn't *do* anything about anything. So we decided we might as well enlarge our raft with all the new empty containers.

Cass went into the Big Top to find a hat. Briquette trotted in behind her and suddenly went bananas—barking furiously, with the hair on the back of her neck standing straight up.

"What is it, Briquette?"

"Come out, Cass!" yelled Rob. "That's her serious bark!"

Everybody ran to the Big Top.

Briquette was going psycho, darting at Cass's sleeping bag. She wouldn't come out, no matter how crossly everybody growled at her. She just ignored us. Briquette can get some weird ideas in her little doggy brain.

Rob grabbed a long stick and fished out Frank's sleeping bag. He flung it outside, then mine, then other bits of our mess. Just as he hooked up Danielle's pajama top, we saw what looked like a piece of shiny black rope.

"*Snake!*"

"*God, there's another one!*"

"*Two* snakes. That's a bit rich, isn't it?"

"Oh, kill the horrible slithery things," said Sue.

"No, don't kill them!" said Zev.

"A copperhead and a red-bellied black snake, I think!" said Rob.

"What are you going to do?"

"Catch them and put them in the bush."

"Rob, you're *not!*" said Donna. "I want this baby to have a father!"

"You're mad!" said Tibor.

"I've seen it done, but I've never actually done it myself," confessed Rob.

So we had a big debate about getting them out, and whether or not we should kill them, and if we did kill them, then how would we do it . . .

But it was all solved by Mr. Nic, who unhooked the tent pegs nearest the bush. Leaning forward and keeping our feet as far away from the tent as possible, we pulled up the guy ropes, lifted the side of the tent, and beat the canvas with a stick. The snakes slithered away, whipping through the grass like fluid lightning.

Briquette went troppo, and it was all Zev and Cass could do to hold her.

"Phew!"

"*Two* Joe Blakes!" said Mr. Nic, running his tongue around the top of his top false teeth.

"And two different *sorts!*" said Sue. "You want to know what I think? I think they were a present from your friend Mad Mattock," said Sue.

"He's your friend, too," said Danielle.

"He's trying to scare us away."

Briquette, the heroine of the hour, was much patted and praised and given extra lunch. She grinned all over her silly face as if she did it all herself.

When the going gets tough, it's time for serious tea-drinking. The parents headed straight for the kettle. Who could have crept in? When? Was there a time when the camp was empty? Was there any fresh evidence?

It was creepy. "Snakes don't stay put for very long," said Rob. "Someone must have been hiding close by, waiting for their chance."

Then Cass and Danielle found two sets of new bootprints on the smooth sand at the river crossing. They were as clear and fresh as though they'd been made with a biscuit cutter. Mad Mattock and son, for sure.

"What do we do now?" said Zev.

"We can't exactly call the cops from way out here."

"We can't call anybody, remember."

"I think we should head home," said Rob. He wanted Donna out of the valley.

"But that's exactly what Mattock *wants* us to do!" said Donna.

"We can't leave that gully till somehow we're sure it's safe!"

Donna had her heart set on describing and classifying every last plant in the rain forest. Tibor had said he'd take photos for her.

"We'll stay," said us kids. We didn't want to run away. No way.

"Oh, sure, with that madman on the rampage," said Rob.

"We can't just ring up the Wilderness Society and say, 'Come and save this precious little gully from Mad Mattock!' There's no one answering the phone. It's the Christmas holidays."

I got rather emotional. "What are we going to do?" I cried. "Leave it to Old Jim to save? He hasn't got a chance. He's an old man. He's all by himself and he's not there now, anyway. We can't just leave. Mattock would be in here in no time with his saws and his bulldozer."

Sue and Mum and Tibor quieted us all down. Some of us had tea and some of us had beer and some of us had a chocolate Big M, then we all felt better.

"It's too late in the day to pack up and leave now, anyway," said Sue, the voice of reason. "So let's sleep on it."

But that was easier said than done. It's fine being brave and volunteering for all kinds of things in the daytime, but I dare you to sleep in a tent after you've seen snakes crawling over your sleeping bag! Not possible.

Zev kept saying that snakes are part of the bush and they are more frightened of *us* than we are of them. Sometimes I think he's from another planet.

"I'm not sleeping in that snake pit," said Frank.

"They've gone, you know."

"I was freaked out of my jocks!" said Danielle.

"You wear knickers," said Cass.

So we all tried to sleep outside on the picnic blankets. Then Frank and Cass were sure they saw a Dulugar or something moving in the bush, and the mosquitoes ate us alive, so we migrated back into the tent. But we still couldn't get to sleep.

"How does Heap do it? He must be eaten alive every night!" said Zev.

Then everyone was asleep except Zev, Cass, Frank, and me. Well, I suppose it *feels* like that when Danielle's asleep.

"It's not fair!" said Cass. "I reckon if Mattock had known which sleeping bag was Danielle's, he would have put both snakes in there, and she's the only one who can get to sleep!"

Then a flashlight came bobbing toward us.

"Move over."

It was Mum with Briquette and her hygienic blanket.

"Now you've got the best watchdog there is. Go to sleep. If you can't go to sleep, we'll *definitely* have to leave here."

Briquette, who was used to "*Get that dog out of your tent,*" couldn't believe her good fortune. She immediately snuffled down in the crook of Frank's legs. Cass fell asleep soon after, with her fingertips just touching Briquette's velvet ear.

25
The Tempest

Next day, the weather was sulking hot. The sky was a gray gold haze, and hot air lay over everything like an invisible electric blanket. (Actually, it *was* an electric blanket, as things turned out!) The moment they were up, the adults went into deep parliamentary debate about Mattock and leaving that day. "You kids buzz off. We'll tell you when we've decided."

We were in the pool, ready to go deaf at the order to start packing. My heart skipped a beat when I saw Dad, Rob, and Sue start up the cars and drive them to the center of the clearing.

Danielle couldn't stand it any longer. "I'm going to find out what's happening." She raced off up the bank.

"We're not leaving," yelled Danielle. "It's too hot." She pointed at the cars. "Fire precaution!"

"Briquette's got a bee in her bonnet," said Rob. "She won't settle, and neither can I. We should have packed up and left ages ago. There's a storm coming, for sure."

We sneaked off to the Talk Rocks with food for Heap. We also tossed over insect repellent. "Thanks," he yelled, but threw it back. "I'm used to 'em now."

By late afternoon, it was even hotter, and the river was the only place to be.

"If I was a tree, I'd drop a branch!" said Sue.

Donna heaved herself around. She had no energy left to go to the gully. She lay on her lounge chair, paddling her feet in the water and reading her thriller.

"Don't worry, Hen. Simply by being here, we're doing something."

Mr. Nic and Tibor dug trenches around the tents, sweating as they bashed the tent pegs in more securely and checked the ropes. Mr. Nic was in his army mood, whistling "Yankee Doodle." We packed up the Reading Room.

The heat continued to build. The clearing was still, and the bush crackled with dryness. The cicadas were quiet. It was even too hot for the insects.

Dinner was mostly stuff out of tins. We talked about people with funny names, and jobs like their names, and how your name affects your life. Rob knew a Mr. Stump who reblocked houses. Tibor said he knew a champion Polish pole-vaulter who gave a very polished performance.

It got dark early. Strangely dark. Spookily dark! And the river turned black. Sue shooed us off to the Arts Council Grant and to clean our teeth. Donna had been nagging Frank to go to bed because he'd been charging along like a steam train all the long hot day. It's always hard for Frank. He keeps up with us pretty well most of the time, but he's younger, and when he's tired, he really goes Captain Collapse.

So we promised Donna we'd at least lie down and play very quiet charades, or something. But a sleeping bag was the last thing in the world you wanted to touch in that heat.

We were cleaning our teeth when a sudden gust of wind swirled a flurry of leaves around us. Plop! Plop! Plop!—huge raindrops the size of grapes hit the dry ground. Stones became speckled eggs.

Then a blinding flash!

CCCRRRAAACCK !

I have *never* been so scared! My toothbrush nearly went through my cheek.

The thunder roared in my bones and my stomach. The ground shook. We ducked and screamed!

Suddenly rain was bucketing down, and everyone was running. A gale whipped us and pulled at the tents. Mum, Dad, and Sue, draped in towels, were throwing things into the cars. Mr. Nic, under his umbrella, was covering his woodpile.

"Get into the tent!" yelled Mum.

"And don't touch the sides, whatever you do!" yelled Rob.

"I didn't rinse!" wailed Cass. The toothpaste down her T-shirt looked like she'd been bombed by a seagull.

CCCRRRAAACCKK!

We screamed again. A deafening clap and splintering as a tree split. "That was close!" yelled Rob.

CRRRAAACCKK!

"This is the best storm!" Zev was grinning, his face lit by lightning, his eyes wide, as if he had magical powers that caused it all. I was terrified for him because of his electric hair. I felt it might draw the lightning to us, so I made him put on his hat.

The sturdy Big Top shook like Jell-O as the wind wrenched at it. Danielle wriggled right down into her sleeping bag and zipped it up until she felt she couldn't breathe anymore, then zipped open a tiny gap and stuck her nose out. We weren't little kids. We didn't cry. We joked bravely and squealed, pretending to be scared when we really were scared. Anyone would have been scared in that storm.

"Okay, kids?" yelled Dad above the drumming of the rain.

"I was just drifting off to sleep . . . was there a noise or something?" yelled Danielle.

CRRRAAACCKK!

136

"AAAAAAAAAAAHHHHHHHHH!" went us kids.

"That was a beauty!" yelled Dad.

I half expected to see our skeletons lit up, like in a cartoon. At home, with a lightning conductor and four strong walls around you, storms don't really matter. You look out the window and there it is. It's exciting, but that's it.

This was pure weather. Just flapping canvas and our sleeping bags between us and it. Everything was tossing, swaying, reeling in the wild roaring gale. Cass squeezed into the sleeping bag with Danielle. Frank clung to me like a frightened monkey.

CRRRAAACCKK,/

As if a bit of the sky has just cracked off. Honestly, you could feel the ground judder! We all rolled together like quivering sardines in the dark, waiting for the next blue-white flash.

Suddenly there was something trying to tear our tent open. We screamed. It yelped. Briquette! Frank unzipped the tent a little, and a wet cannonball flew straight into Zev's sleeping bag.

"Ahhhhh! Get out, you soggy dog."

Danielle and Cass wrapped her in a towel and somehow squeezed her in with them.

"She's absolutely quivering!"

CRRRAAACCKK!

Briquette thrashed and whimpered.

"Ow! She scratched me!"

CRRRAAACCKK.!

The thunder was moving a little farther off.

"It's going!"

"What about Heap?" Zev said suddenly.

"He hasn't got a tent."

"More bad luck."

"Imagine this on your own. Oh, that would be so scary. I reckon he's brave."

"He might sleep through it."

"You're kidding. Not even Heap could sleep through this."

CRRAACCKK!

"What will we do if he's not there tomorrow?"

Nobody spoke for a bit.

"Oh, I wish I was a bunnykins in a snug warm burrow."

"Then the water would flood in and drown you."

"Is that what happens to rabbits?"

"Burrows don't have little watertight doors."

"What if you were a bird?"

"Put your head under your wing and hang on tight."

"Imagine being a sailor. At sea. That would be the worst. No safe place."

"Ooooh, I want to go to the toilet," said Cass.

CRR RAAACCK!

"No, I don't!"

"Wonder if the lightning trees have been hit. I bet Old Jim's sitting on his veranda, watching the fireworks."

"There's no way they could get a bulldozer in here now. At least the gully's safe, for the moment."

"Hello in there!" Rob and Dad were prowling around, checking things.

"We're scared!" we said.

"So are we!"

The thunder growled away, like a huge barrel rolling off around the distant mountains. We counted between the flashes and the rumbles. The time got longer and longer. We zipped up our sleeping bags, because the temperature had dropped, and lay there, listening to the drumming rain. Not talking, for once. And one by one, we all fell asleep.

26
After the Storm

We woke up to a gray morning with gentle rain. Branches were down, and twigs and leaves were strewn everywhere as if someone had turned the bush upside down and shaken it furiously, like a terrier shakes a rat. The ground was a full sponge. Water squished out when you put your foot down.

It was steady rain, ordinary, dropping straight down. It sounded like a never-ending sigh.

"Everybody make it through the night?" yelled Rob.

"We didn't!" yelled Danielle.

"Anybody wet?" yelled Dad.

"I'm soggerized!" yelled Cass. "My sleeping bag was against the side."

"Anybody cold?" yelled Mum.

"No."

"Where's Briquette?" yelled Donna.

"Here!" we chorused.

"Can you get room service?" yelled Tibor.

"Only if you're Donna," yelled Rob.

"Donna, how are you both?" yelled Dad.

"We're okay, but there's a tree somewhere close by that's been made into matches."

"Yes. What a cracker of a storm. All those fireworks for free!"

Rob put on his old raincoat and sneakers and padded around the place, checking things out. *"I love a sunburned country . . .* Actually, it's not all that cold." Then there was a shout from farther away: "My GOD!"

"What is it?"

"The river! You won't *believe* it!"

That got us going. We scrambled into our bathing suits and thongs and sloshed outside.

"WOW!"

Our friendly pool was a raging river. Like a powerful brown serpent, it tore at the banks. Branches and clumps of earth and debris swept along in the torrent and snagged against Government Rocks. The stone beach was gone, Bird Poo Island was gone, the rope across the river, our drawings, and our shops were deep under the swirling water.

"Like the lost city of Atlantis," said Zev.

Small rivers ran everywhere, feeding into the big river. Mr. Nic's firewood had a mini creek trickling through it, but the cover was still on.

"In this whole wet place, the only things dry are inside the tents, inside the cars, and Mr. Nic's wood," said Frank.

Rob squelched back from the ford. "Maroooned! We're all

marooooned! I hope the ford is still there when the river goes down."

I was so happy. My fear for the gully relaxed, like when you haven't finished your school project and you go to school and your teacher is away sick.

It started to rain more heavily, so we went back to the Big Top. Cass squished off to the Arts Council Grant, with the umbrella.

"This is very tricky!" she yelled. "And the toilet paper's a sog!"

She brought it back with her.

"When it stops raining, we should unroll it and dry it out on the bushes," said Frank, but Cass was already ripping off chunks and making papier-mâché animals.

27
The Stella Street Tribe

Be prepared for a poetic bit, because I can still remember this as clear as crystal, and it can't be told in any other way if I'm to do the telling. And it's surprising, so when it happens suddenly to you, that's how it was for us. It's also rather gory.

Rain drifted across the mountains all morning. The weather was gray and closed-in, and so were we. We played cards in the Big Top: Spit, Strip Jack Naked, Clean Nose, and good old Spoons. Mr. Nic played Spoons, too, in a totally hopeless way. We knew he'd be first out because he was sitting on a stool and couldn't even reach the spoons. Sometimes, Zev and I read.

Even Danielle was pleased to see Heap at the Talk Rocks. He wore a tatty gray groundsheet around his shoulders. He looked more like a caveman than ever, with his long wet hair plastered to his head.

"Were you okay in the storm?" yelled Zev.

"Got a bit wet!" But he wasn't miserable. "How's Donna?" He didn't even ask to see her.

Throwing the food over was dangerous, because our Talk Rock had become a slippery island and Zev had to jump onto it. I threw the container up to Zev, and he threw it over to Heap, who waved thanks.

The adults moved into the Big Top, too, because it was the only dry place where you could stand up and be comfortable. They sat near the door, talking—mostly about how places became national parks—drinking tea, reading, and watching the showers drip down.

It was not long after morning tea when, out of the blue, Donna leaped up with a squeak as if she'd left her bag on the tram. It all began with that little squeak.

"What? What have you remembered?"

"Somebody's coming to join us!"

"Nobody's going to get over that river," said Rob in a matter-of-fact voice, turning a page, "so you can stop making scones."

"No," said Donna. "I'm *leaking.*"

Tibor looked at the tent above her.

"No! Not the tent . . . *me!*"

"*Cripes!*" Mr. Nic understood in a flash. You should have seen his face! Dead white!

"Holy *mackerel!*" said Rob, leaping up.

Mum gasped. "Are you sure?"

"Positive!" said Donna, biting her bottom lip like a naughty little girl who was told not to do something and then did it.

The parents sat, stunned. We stopped our game and listened.

"I've been having contractions, just little friendly 'hello' ones, since before sunrise, and I *thought* they were Braxton Hicks, but . . . just now . . ." She pointed to her right leg. A trickle of clear liquid was running down to a pool at her heel. "My water has broken!"

"What?" said Cass. "How can water break?"

"What? What's happening?" said Frank.

"Can someone tell us what's happening?" said Danielle.

"I'm going to have the baby," said Donna quietly. "Here."

"Oh my God!" Rob hugged her. "There's no way we could get you across the river. We'd be bogged on the track, then it's another twelve miles to town, even if we could get you to the road."

"What?" said Frank. "Are you going to have the baby *now*?"

"Not this instant. It will probably take hours," said Sue. At last, someone was talking to us! "But the baby's starting to be born. That 'water' is what the baby's been floating in all these months."

"Could we fetch a doctor or midwife?" asked Tibor. (I remember him saying "fetch.")

Dad shook his head. "We're cut off. Totally! Stranded. Rob tried his cell phone again this morning. Nothing. We may as well be on the moon."

"The storm, Donna!" said Sue. "The drop in barometric pressure's set you off."

"It's a natural process, you know," said Donna cheerfully, almost as if she had put on the worried act so they wouldn't be cross with her. "Babies are born all over the world in lots of strange places. I could have had the baby at home. And this is much better than the back of a taxi, don't you think?"

"You have no choice," said Rob.

So that was how it all began, with Donna jollying everyone along. Us kids had no idea what would happen, but we thought it was very exciting.

"Are you hungry, Donna?" asked Mum.

"Yes. Tell you what I fancy: macaroni and pickles and a cup of tea with sugar!"

"You *never* have sugar!" said Rob.

"I do today," said Donna.

But it was an early lunch—tin of soup, 2 Minute Noodles, things from packets. Nobody could concentrate.

"'The birth will go more smoothly if the mother has confidence in herself and can relax,'" read Rob from the baby book.

"Fine," said Donna.

"... blah blah blah ... 'shave off pubic hair and have an enema ...'"

"Skip that bit," said Donna.

"What's public hair?" asked Frank.

Cass pointed to where it grew.

"That should be called *private* hair!" said Frank indignantly.

"Tibor, lend us your watch to time the contractions," said Rob.

"What contraptions?" asked Frank.

"I've already *told* you," said Rob.

"Let me have a go," said Sue, taking a deep breath. "Contractions. Baby Watermelon is inside and wants to come out. Now, the special hole near Donna's bottom has to get big enough for a baby to fit through . . ."

Danielle giggled.

"Shut up!" said Frank.

"Don't you laugh at my bottom!" said Donna. "Anyway, it's nearer the front."

"Okay," said Sue. "Donna's stomach muscles have to pull open that hole. And when they pull, that's called a contraction. Gradually, after a lot of contractions, the hole becomes big enough for the baby's head to slip through."

Then Mum had a go. "Contractions feel sort of like powerful waves inside you. They build up and fade away, build up and fade away. You can't control them, they just happen. They get stronger and stronger, with less time in between, until finally they push the baby out into the world."

148

"And they get painful," said Donna.

"You wanted a drug-free birth!" said Rob.

Sue and Mum glanced at each other, and Mum raised her eyebrows one millimeter.

"Do you take *drugs* when you have a baby?" Frank looked worried.

"Sometimes you need them to stop the pain."

Danielle piped up, "Claire's mum said it was like pooping a melon."

Dad glared at her.

Mr. Nic said, "I'll just go and check that fire," which was a funny thing to say, because there wasn't a fire.

"I was just telling you what she said!" protested Danielle.

Then Tibor, whose manners are perfect, said something wise. "Danielle's right. This is not the time for silly talk but for honest talk. This is a rough place to have a baby, and we have to say what we think. A lot of things that might be rude in other places will not be rude today. It's not a normal day."

Donna straightened up and rubbed her back. "Another thing, kids. You know what I always say about swearing?"

"Yep. No swearing," said Cass.

"Oh, we wouldn't swear. No way. Especially not today," said Zev.

"Well, *I'm* allowed to swear today," said Donna. "If you're having a baby, it's okay. You can do whatever helps."

Mum, Sue, and Donna tried to remember all they could about the birth of their babies—us! And Rob read the baby book.

"We'll need clean warm towels to wrap around the little body when it comes out," said Sue, switching into practical mode.

"We don't have clean towels," said Mum, grimacing. "We don't have clean *anything*. Everything's got a week of grime on it."

"I'll check with Mr. Nic," said Cass, shooting out of the tent. Our reliable secret weapon, Mr. Nic! He had a towel he hadn't used and a clean white cotton shirt in a plastic bag, "Just in case I needed to look smart."

"My new Tokyo Shock Boys T-shirt's clean at the bottom of my pack," said Zev.

"Kids, we want Donna to have the Big Top, where there's space to move around," said Dad. "We need to make it as comfortable and pleasant as possible."

"I'll have my chair, my pillow, and our Lilo," said Donna. "I'm Lady Muck today."

Luckily, it had stopped raining. We shoved our stuff into our bags and put them in the cars, and the rest of our gear into Rob and Donna's yellow tent.

Mr. Nic was down at the fireplace trying to start a fire.

"Sorry about what I said, Mr. Nic," said Danielle.

"I'm not too clever with all that," said Mr. Nic, and his chin trembled.

We just stood there. We couldn't think of what to say. The eternally cheerful Mr. Nic was sniffing and blinking.

"Got to get this fire going." Then he was busy cracking sticks and crumpling paper. "Took me back, that's all. Yes. Took me back. You see, we wanted babies. Oh my goodness, we wanted babies." He wiped his eyes on his shirt and redoubled his efforts. "Got to get this fire going."

"Okay, Mr. Stick, we'll go and get some nicks for you—some sticks for you," said Frank.

"Good man."

And we ran off. Oh, poor, poor Mr. Nic. We'd always known him as good old ever-cheerful Mr. Nic. We knew he'd had a wife who died a long time ago. Maybe that was why he liked kids and animals and birds so much.

"I've got a job for you lot." Rob strode up with Briquette bouncing along behind. "Keep Briquette away. We don't want her underfoot today."

Of course, Briquette knew immediately that she wasn't wanted, and her whole aim in life became to get into the Big Top and, if possible, to sit on Donna. Briquette became "that dog," as in "Get 'that dog' away!"

Apart from bossing Briquette, there wasn't much for us kids to do. Between showers, we went to the riverbank, where we marked the edge of the water with sticks to see if it was still rising. It was—slightly.

From time to time, we visited Donna. The Big Top was transformed. We had to take our thongs off when we went inside. The carpet had been swept and was bright again. The big blue groundsheet had been washed down with antiseptic and put over Rob and Donna's luxury Lilo, with a sheet over the top of that, and there was a stack of pillows. But Donna was still walking around.

"It helps if I lean on something during the contractions," she said. "Whoops. Here we go again." She held on to the pole in the center of the Big Top, rested her head on her hands, closed her eyes, and breathed slowly.

"Why is she breathing like that?" whispered Cass.

"It helps her relax," said Sue. "She tries to think about the breathing, not the pain."

Donna had contractions for hours. Sue was steady and calm. She was the only one who had done a first-aid course. Her fine hands were bare, and when Sue takes off her rings, she means business. Mum, the quiet achiever, was her assistant. They were like three sisters.

Dad was a little too jolly and kept to himself more than usual. This was something he couldn't organize.

"Please don't," I heard Sue say quietly about something, and whatever Dad was going to do, he didn't. So I understood that the women were the main ones that day. Dad made cups of tea and passed around biscuits.

Tibor said, "Please tell me if I can help." He washed things and rigged up clotheslines by the fire, and when he couldn't think of anything else to do, he sat in the car and read.

Then, watching Sue and Mum, I saw a sharp anxious look flicker between them. That was when I caught the fear. It was an exciting and frightening fear. A shared fear, like we were a tribe—the Stella Street tribe.

I don't know what the adults were thinking at that time, but I had read so many books and seen so many films where the mother died when the baby was born. They never tell you what the problem was. It's always the doctor coming out of the room, drying his hands, with a downcast look on his face, saying, "I'm afraid I was too late."

Then the father goes, "And the baby . . . ?"

Then the nurse comes out holding a bundle, and says, "Your beautiful son, Mr. So-and-So."

Later in the day, it became a dull steady fear that went on and on. We were all part of a big risk for two of the most precious lives in the world—to us. Cass slipped the Heart of the Pool in her pocket, sure it would bring good luck.

It was a very, very long day. Briquette got so restless, not being able to run around. Sometimes we'd be drawing or doing something for half an hour, and we'd forget what was happening. Then we'd remember.

"Is the baby here yet?" asked Frank, as if it was a parcel someone was delivering.

"Not yet," said Donna wearily.

"Can I listen to the baby's heart?" Frank asked.

While he was listening, Donna had a contraction. "Hey! It's getting faster . . . it's *really* fast . . . now it's slowing down."

Rob sat beside Donna. Sue talked to her quietly, encouraging her through the contractions. Donna was totally focused on the breathing.

"Donna, can we . . . well . . . do you mind . . . um . . ." Then I thought of what Tibor had said about honest talk. "Can we watch the baby being born?"

"I don't know," said Donna. "I'll tell you later. Oh God. I'd forgotten how much it hurts! Oh, this is cramping all right," said Donna. "Rub my back just here, sweet."

Mr. Nic stayed beside the fire. I don't know what was going on in his mind, but he certainly was busy at that fire. Tibor's lines and racks were covered with washing, and Mr. Nic was turning things around as if his life depended on drying them.

"When's the baby going to come?" asked Frank.

"It takes a long time," said Mum. "Why don't you do some drawings for Donna."

So we squashed into the yellow tent and went to work on the painkiller drawings.

"Remember she likes bright colors," said Frank.

"Pictures for a bush baby," said Zev.

"A storm boy?" I said.

"A storm girl?" said Danielle.

"A tentacle," said Cass.

"They're great!" said Donna. Then her lips went thin, and her face went tight, and she breathed in this steady way, almost as if she was in a trance, staring at Frank's blue elephant drawing. Then the contraction died away and she became normal again. "That blue elephant helped. Make them strong and simple."

So we gave up on the sunsets, hills, and beaches. The one Donna found best when the pain was really hard was Cass's drawing of the big fiddleback tree.

I think Dad must have made a hundred cups of tea that day. Every time I saw him, he was lining up the mugs.

We made yet another visit to Donna, but this time things had changed.

"Out of the way!" said Sue.

We squashed into the corner of the tent, quiet as mice. They forgot about us. I had Frank on my knee, and when we saw Donna's face all screwed up, and heard her groaning really deep down low, like a wounded animal, I thought he might start to cry, but he had his eyes closed and his fingers in his ears. Everyone was anxious.

Donna was sitting in her chair. "I want to squat!" she said, groaning urgently. "I want to lean on something. Oh God! I want to squat! I want to push! Oh God." She was crumpling at the knees.

"Steady! Steady, Donna darling. Lean on us!"

"Quick, get the big coolers, *the big coolers!*" Sue shouted.

I have never seen Rob and Dad move so fast.

Donna was panting and half-crying and groaning.

"The head! Pant, Donna! Pant! Pant like a dog! Let the head out slowly," said Sue.

And at long last, bracing herself between the two big coolers, with her friends all around her, Donna gave birth. The little boy slipped out. First his head, then his shoulders, then the rest of him just slithered out with a flood of the liquid that had been around him. He gave a squeaky little meowing sound.

Rob was half-lying on the ground with his arms outstretched, and he caught his little boy with such gentleness in his big hands.

Oh, the wonder of that baby! We saw it all. He became alive in the air, in our world, with us. The little fingers moving, hands waving around, tiny little fingernails the size of a grain of wheat. We saw his first blink, his first breath, heard his first noise, first hiccup, first gurgle, first snuffle, the first time he felt the air. He was totally new. His little pink sausage legs gave a kick, and his cheeks were chubby.

Sue carefully wiped around his nose and eyes and checked him all over—to see if he was all there, I suppose.

We just looked and looked and soaked it up. We were all whispering.

"One of the ears is bent!"

"That'll straighten out."

"His hair's stuck to his head."

"Why is he all waxy?" whispered Zev.

"Vernix," said Mum, "helps him slide out. Kept him from getting wrinkly in the water inside."

Tibor chuckled quietly. "I once bought a car engine preserved in wax."

The little baby squinted at us.

"Hello, son!" said Rob.

"Hello, brother," said Frank. "You look like a big pink frog."

"Look at the cord," whispered Cass, "it's like wet twisted rope."

The cord ran from the baby's middle to inside Donna.

"Reminds me of a spaceman, you know, with the tube going back to the mother ship."

We just looked and looked.

"What do you think?" said Donna. She was so happy.

"He's lovely."

"I'm going to cut the cord," said Rob.

My scissors had been boiled in honor of the job.

"Gosh, it's rubbery," said Rob. "Just as well it doesn't hurt."

With Tibor's finest string, he tied the cord twice, once close to the baby's middle, then along about two inches toward Donna.

Snip! He cut between.

"Okay! You're on your own now, my little son. And you've got a belly button."

"Knock, knock. I'd like to come in, if I may." It was Mr. Nic. "I believe congratulations are in order!" He presented Donna with a bunch of delicate gum branches in a ketchup bottle. He gazed at the baby. "And to think they called you a watermelon!"

"And this is for the baby, from us," said Cass. She slipped the Heart of the Pool from her pocket and gave it to Donna. She hadn't asked us, and it was the best of our treasures, but it was right.

Then Donna eased back onto the big Lilo and Mum packed her around with pillows. Then Sue put the little baby straight on Donna's tummy, then onto her breast, and do you know what? The little gobble-guts started drinking! Right then!

"He's witchetty grubbish," said Cass.

"He's perfect," said Donna.

28
A Hitch

Now here's an important bit of information. You probably think that when a woman has a baby, that's all she has. But no! She has a baby *and* a placenta.

After the baby was born, we were all crazy happy, laughing and joking. Donna was always sure it was going to be a boy, so it was almost not a surprise.

"You really were Lady Muck," said Cass, watching Sue and Tibor mopping up.

"He had a big swimming pool," said Sue.

"You didn't swear much, Donna," said Zev.

"Didn't I? Oh, I'm so glad I was dignified!"

"I forgot to ask if you wanted beer in the coolers or not," said Rob.

I suppose it was about three quarters of an hour later when Sue said, "The placenta still hasn't come out."

"What's the play center?" asked Frank.

Everyone laughed.

"It's a Fisher-Price activity center with twiddly things for the baby to play with inside when it's bored," said Rob.

"Don't listen to him," growled Sue. "It's where the baby's oxygen and food come from while it's growing inside the womb."

"It looks like McDonald's!" said Rob.

We went on joking, but all the mothers remembered the placenta coming out quite soon after their babies were born.

"It's still in there."

"What do we do?"

"Reach in and grab it?"

"What would the Aborigines have done in the bush? They'd have had some herbal brew."

"Chew on a gum leaf?"

Donna was exhausted. She gave a weak white-faced smile. "I don't care what you do. I'm just going to lie here with my little darling boy."

Nothing was wrong, exactly, but it hadn't finished. Donna was very sore where the baby had came out, and she was bleeding from up inside.

"'The placenta follows shortly after.'" Rob stared at the page. "Shortly? Shortly? What do they mean by shortly? This book's bloody hopeless."

Sue hushed him.

"If something goes wrong at this stage, she might start hemorrhaging. If she really starts bleeding . . . ," murmured Rob.

"Don't even *think* about it," whispered Mum.

So the fear grew again, and we really knew it when Dad said, "How would you kids like to read quietly in your tent for a while?"

29
Zev's Idea

We sat in the yellow tent, squashed up, worried, and crabby, with Briquette chewing her leash.

"You don't think Donna might . . ."

"If you say anything to upset Frank," I hissed at Danielle, "I'll boil you."

Zev was fiddling with his walkie-talkie. "I've got an idea," he said slowly, "but there's one big problem. We'll need Heap."

Danielle groaned.

"Go on, Zev. Go *on!*"

"Where does Rob keep the cell phone?"

"In the glove box," said Cass. She was out of the tent in a flash.

It's amazing how hope can come back so fast.

"We're in a valley here, so *we* can't get a signal, but I think the phone would work from the top of the big ridge," said Zev.

"The river's too deep to cross. But *Heap's* on the other side."

Cass darted in, breathless. "Here it is. They're all in the Big Top, except Mr. Nic's back at the fire."

We sneaked to the Talk Rocks with their backdrop of wet dripping bush.

"Oh, this is hopeless. He won't be around," said Cass.

"*HEEEEEEEEAP!*" I yelled. "*HEEEEEEEEAP!*" we all yelled. "*HEEEEEEEEEEEEEEEEEEEEAP!*"

To our amazement, Heap came out of the bush almost immediately, wrapped in the tatty groundsheet. I'd never been so pleased to see that ragged figure.

"He's been watching us," hissed Danielle.

"Why have you got the big fire?" he yelled. "Why's the dog tied up? What's all the fuss? What's going on?"

"Donna's had her baby!"

"*Ah, great!*" He grinned. "What sort?"

"A little boy."

"*Ah, great!*"

"But there's a problem," said Zev. "We need your help."

"Sure," said Heap.

"I'm going to throw this walkie-talkie to you."

Immediately, Heap didn't look so sure. He peered down at the brown torrent surging between the rocks.

"Pretend it's food. Okay? Get ready. Here it comes."

Zev's throw was good, but Heap fumbled. With an awful *clunk*, the walkie-talkie hit the wet rock and began to slide. He just grabbed it and nearly lost his balance. If he'd gone into the river, he would have been swept away for sure. When I heard that *clunk*, I got the awful sick feeling again.

Danielle was breathing loudly through gritted teeth. I gave her the fiercest look I've ever looked. She did a low growl at me.

Zev's face was set. "Okay, Heap. Try it. The knob turns it on, and press the button to talk. Zev to Heap? Zev to Heap? Can you hear me?" Zev shouted into his walkie-talkie. We could see Heap fiddling and listening, fiddling and listening.

Nothing.

"Zev to Heap? Zev to Heap?"

Nothing.

"Don't call me Heap!" yelled Heap, flustered and angry. "My name's Clay."

This was a *total* surprise. I nearly slipped off my rock. We thought his real name was Marcus. Everyone always called him Heap.

"Okay, Clay!" Zev was so cool. When he goes for something, he really goes for it. He never called him Heap again. "Zev to Clay? Zev to Clay? Can you hear me?"

"No."

I thought Zev's brilliant idea had come to nothing. Poor

Donna was lying there in danger, and nobody knew what to do. I felt paralyzed. But not Zev.

"Okay, Clay, throw it back!"

Carefully, Heap tossed. Heap, Clay. I still get it wrong!

The black shape flew over the river, and Zev caught it easily.

"Good one. Now I'm going to throw over the other walkie-talkie. Okay? Clay?"

"Yes."

Clay braced himself with his feet apart and his hands ready, like a kid who's just learned to catch. Zev tossed. Clay held it up and grinned. "Got it!"

"What's the use of one walkie-talkie?" said Danielle.

Zev flipped the batteries out of the dropped walkie-talkie, took three combs from his pocket, stuck his thumb and a wiry thing in the battery space, and began to flick the combs quickly through his hair.

"Zev to Clay? Zev to Clay?"

"Yes! I can hear you."

Even from where we were, we could hear loud crackling, but these rocks were only twenty feet apart. Would it work over a greater distance? And how long could Zev's electricity last?

Zev held up the cell phone.

"Clay, now I'm going to throw over this phone. It's heavy!"

Clay looked worried, but nodded. He didn't understand what

was going on. He just followed Zev's instructions. Cass couldn't watch. It was too excruciating.

Zev tossed. In its slow-motion flight, the phone seemed to pause in the air—like us on the rope swing. Then Heap brought his hands together on it, as if in prayer.

"*Yes!* Good one, Clay!"

"Fantastic, Heap, Clay, Cleap! Hay! Whatever!" we cheered.

Clay looked slightly terrified. He had never held a cell phone before. Zev told him how to use it, and Clay repeated the instructions.

"Practice that for a sec," yelled Zev.

"Quick, Hen, set your watch on half past six!" said Zev, adjusting his own. With a bit of a fiddle, we got both watches on precisely the same time.

"Clay, I'm going to throw my watch over."

Another neat piece of technology was flung over the river.

"Clay," yelled Zev, "now *listen*. The phone might work from the top of the ridge. Go right to the top and dial 000. That's emergency. Ask for a doctor or midwife. It's *urgent*. Tell them a lady's had a baby and the placenta hasn't come out. Ask them what we should do."

"What's it called again?"

"The placenta."

"The *play center*," yelled Frank.

"How long will it take you to get up there?" asked Zev.

"Half an hour. It's wet. Longer."

"Clay, it's *urgent*. I'll call you on the walkie-talkie at seven o'clock, then you can tell us what they say. If you can't hear me, make the phone call anyway, then come back and tell us."

Zev went through it all again with him. Clay nearly dropped the watch, putting it on his wrist, but finally he was ready.

"Good luck, Clay."

He climbed down from the rock and looked straight at us for a moment. Then he ran into the dripping bush.

"It won't work," said Danielle. "He can't do it. He'll muck it up for sure. It's silly even trying."

No one replied to her.

"Clay!" she scoffed. "Do you reckon his name is Clay? I bet he made that up."

"Will you *shut up*, Danielle," snapped Cass.

"It's a chance! We've got to keep hoping!" I was fighting back tears.

"He'll do it," said Zev.

I think I saw every second of that half hour on my watch. We looked at the swirling brown water and tried to think of ways to get across it. Zev wondered about doctors and helicopters.

"Thirty seconds to go!" I said. Zev arranged his combs.

. . . Four, three, two, one.

He began to comb furiously. "Zev to Clay? Zev to Clay? Over?" His face was sharp, then suddenly it snapped into joy. "YES! . . . GREAT! . . . YES! . . . THE STOMACH . . . YES! . . . (He was going like a combing machine! I thought his hair would catch fire!) YES! . . . PINK! . . . ALL THERE . . . RIGHT! . . . YES! . . . ZEV TO CLAY? ZEV TO CLAY?"

"Lost him," said Zev, "but I've got it! Don't talk. Have to remember it."

We ran like the wind to the Big Top.

"What's going on?" growled Rob when we burst in.

"Listen to Zev!" I pleaded.

Zev stood there with a half-silly grin on his face, holding up his walkie-talkie. "Don't worry, it will come out. She said rub the top of her stomach. That helps it. And she says make sure it *all* comes out. That's very important. And she wanted to know what color the baby was. It's okay! We don't have to worry!"

"Who said? Who is this? What are you talking about?" Sue grabbed Zev's arm.

"A proper midwife. Someone on the other side of the river took the cell phone to the top of the ridge and rang a midwife for us. It's okay!"

Rob wrapped his big arms around Zev and nearly squashed him flat.

"Who took the phone?" asked Dad, amazed.

"Tell us later." Sue began to massage Donna's stomach.

Donna groaned, then, as if it had been waiting for this one last contraction, the gooey, redder-than-liver, yuk, sloppy-looking, spongy, wet, shiny, soft, big *thing*, with veins over it, slipped out of Donna.

"Is it all there?" Sue cupped it in her hands. "The cord, the membranes? Is it all out?"

"I think so. I think so."

"It reminds me of the foot of a piece of seaweed, where it hangs on to the rock," I said.

"Hello, placenta! Boy, are we glad to see you!" said Cass.

We all had a good look at this thing that had caused so much worry; then Sue put it in a plastic bag.

"Some tribes eat the placenta," said Rob. "It's a custom. Rich in vitamins and minerals."

"The Stella Street tribe doesn't," said Donna firmly.

"Now, who took the phone to the top of the ridge?" asked Tibor.

"Heap."

"You're *kidding!*" said Donna. "Up *here?*"

"Except he's called Clay now," said Cass.

"I can't believe this vacation," said Mum. "It's one extraordinary thing after another."

"And he spoke to the *midwife?*" said Donna. "On the *cell phone?*"

"Yep."

Out came the full Don't Stress Donna story of Heap and the food and the Talk Rocks.

Donna smiled as she shook her head, marveling. "He's a tough one!"

We went back to the Talk Rocks several times to tell Heap—*Clay*—the good news, but he didn't turn up. Then it was dark.

It was a little while after that, when the baby gave a gurgle and a little snuffly noise, that Donna's chin began to tremble; then she started to cry. Happiness or relief or worry? I honestly don't know what it was, but we all started to howl. Anyone coming across us would have thought we were some mad howling tribe. Even *Dad*! Sobbing and sniffing and laughing and blowing our noses. Tears streamed down Sue's cheeks. Kissing and hugging. Rob wiped his eyes on Mum's skirt. Mr. Nic fogged up his glasses. Briquette, who was still where we tied her near the bend in the river, heard the strange noises and started to howl, which made us even worse! It was incredible!

"Who wants a cup of tea?" said Dad for the two hundredth time. Deep breaths all around. The gales of tears subsided, and feeling a bit foolish, but very happy, we mopped ourselves up.

Now, when we tell people the story of the birth, we always finish by saying, "Then we all had a good cry!"

So Dad made the last cup of tea for the day and offered round the Arnott's Family Pack of cookies, and us kids stirred heaped spoonfuls of powdered milk and chocolate syrup into a thick mud and added hot water. Then we sat around in the Big Top, like the shepherds and the Wise Men around Mary and Jesus and Joseph. And Frank sneaked Briquette in. We all had one last look at the baby. Our baby.

When we finally tiptoed out, being so quiet and polite and leaving the little family alone, Tibor was the last to leave. He forgot to let down the flap, and Rob called out, "Hey! Were you born in a tent?"

It always makes us laugh.

30
The Day Between

We all slept soundly. We were ab—so—lute—ly exhausted. I missed the birds' chorus.

The day was clear and mild, with a little breeze. After the storm and the birth day, it all seemed light and peaceful and calm. How days like this mock human life. After a battle in wartime, if your friends had died, a beautiful morning like this would be so unfair. What a cruel day this would have been if something had gone wrong with the baby. I don't know why I thought like this. I just did.

But the little baby, wrapped in the Tokyo Shock Boys T-shirt, was sleeping soundly in the strong pineapple carton Sue had used to pack food. He fitted so neatly in the box, Donna immediately called him "my little pineapple."

"He sleeps a lot," said Frank.

"You would, too, if you'd been through what he's been through," said Donna.

"He's got birth lag," said Danielle.

"Baby Pineapple, born on the Warrangalla," read Dad from an imaginary newspaper. "Mother, baby, and placenta doing well."

"What did you do with my lovely placenta?" asked Donna.

"I'm cooking it in a white wine sauce with garlic for your breakfast," said Rob. "No. I risked my life at the creek, took it to the gully, and buried it among the blackwoods."

Donna smiled at that.

The big surprise came when we went to feed Clay. There on his Talk Rock was a STONE! And beside it, in a plastic bag, the phone, the walkie-talkie, and the watch.

"Yesss! Yip! Yip! *Yay!*" went Danielle. "He's gone!"

"Danielle, you ungrateful little ratbag," I yelled at her. "He was *fantastic*! He found out about the placenta."

"It would have come out anyway," she said.

The river started to drop. We watched it go down, marking the edge every hour. We cleaned up the stony beach as it reappeared. Fallen branches had made branch jams against rocks, with fern fronds and grass and sticks. We wanted to have one more swim before we left.

The mother and her little boy slept most of the day. The others walked back along the track a couple of times to see if the ford was passable. It soon was—the river went down as fast as it came up.

"We could move out as soon as Donna's up to it," said Rob. "She's still bleeding a bit, but she's not worried about it."

"That's normal," said Sue. "I think I bled for about ten days or so."

Later on, Sue and Mum took Donna downstream to a spot in the rocks where she could have a wash and put on clean clothes. They were her handmaidens, like the ones you see in those big oil paintings of gods and goddesses.

It was a quiet day. Briquette had her freedom again, and Zev had a comb-sore head.

The Stella Street tribe talked of packing up and leaving, the danger of getting bogged in the mud, fresh food, TV, movies, and newspapers. Mum and Dad half-packed some boxes. Our thoughts had turned toward home.

I knew Rob and Donna wanted to be where it was easier to look after the little boy. We all wanted to go, but what about the gully? The baby had become more important than the fiddleback tree, though we didn't want to compare such things. And I know it was totally unreasonable, but I felt Donna had somehow let the gully down.

My fear for the fiddleback tree came seeping back. What

would happen when we left? I lay on my Lilo, worrying.

That night I had a nightmare. The sun had become our enemy, but I couldn't make anyone understand. I was shouting and shouting, trying to warn everybody that the sun was evil.

I woke myself up. Then I started thinking about the gully, and I began to cry quietly. I cried myself to sleep, being careful not to get my sleeping bag wet. See, even when I'm absolutely miserable, I'm still sensible!

31
A Splash in the Water

Everyone else was still asleep. Cass was snuffling occasionally. I knew this was the day we would leave. I told myself, "I'm nearly twelve years old and I'm starting junior high school this year, and I'm not going to let this tree business worry me."

Then, as the light grew stronger and the sun became golden through the trees and the birds began their morning chorus, my fear changed to a feeling of determination. As soon as we got to a telephone, I was going to ring the prime minister, the Wilderness Society, Greenpeace, the Conservation Foundation, Midnight Oil, and Friends of the Earth. *Somebody* must be answering their phone in the Christmas holidays.

Then I decided that Rob, Tibor, and Dad had to go to the sawmill and talk to Mattock. (Mattock wouldn't listen to women and children. He thought men were always the boss.) Then Dad and Mattock would have an argument. Dad would get steamed up, then something would *really* happen. (I didn't know what, but if Dad gets mad . . . ! That's where Danielle gets it from.) But Danielle mustn't be anywhere in sight, otherwise Mattock would burst a blood vessel!

I felt much better. Then the alarm clock bird went off: *da da da da . . . da da da da . . . da da da da. . . .* I laughed. Imagine being an alarm clock bird all your life!

When the others woke up, I tried to tell them about my sun nightmare, which I could remember quite clearly, and my plans for action, but they were sleepy and not in the mood to listen.

"You worry too much," said Danielle.

"You don't worry enough," I snapped.

I took myself off and sat by the river.

Dear God,
Why can't they see how important this is?
Do writers worry more? Would you please
ask Roald Dahl if that's the case. Is he up
there? He didn't seem the worrying type.
How did he do it? Ask him. And ask him
what he'd do about the gully.
    Yours,
        Mixed-up but determined.
            Henni

Splash! A rock hit the water in front of me! I got such a fright I nearly fell in.

"Henni! Henni! Henni!" It was Heap, on the other side of the river, waving frantically, hitting his fist against his leg and jigging as if he had a terrible rash and couldn't keep still. I'd never seen him move quickly like that before. "There's a bulldozer on the track on the ridge above the gully!"

Mattock's come for the fiddleback tree! My stomach turned. My legs felt wobbly. Then a voice in my head said, "You wanted to do something, Henni Octon. Well, *do* it!"

I flew to the tent and grabbed my boots. "There's a BULLDOZER above the gully!"

Zev scrambled for his clothes.

"I'm going *now!*" I shouted. We were so squashed in that tent, I knew the others would take ages to find their boots.

The bushes along the river track whipped me as I raced toward the gully. I could hear the blood pounding in my head. Then a black shadow bounded up behind me. "Briquette!"

The creek was over the track, so I quickly took off my boots and waded through.

"It's *icy*, Briquette," I gasped. She put two paws in, then backed out. I was tying my laces when Zev caught up. Boy, was I glad to see him.

"Shhhh! In case they're in the gully!"

We climbed as quietly as we could into the dripping rain forest, wet from brushing through the ferns. We stopped to listen—just the sounds of the bush. The big blackwood trees stood as they had for centuries.

"On one of those maps, there was a path up this side, I think."

"It's pretty steep," said Zev, "and slippery."

"The others will take ages."

Then we heard, "Wait! Wait for us! *Wait!*"

"How can we do *anything* with them?" I groaned.

The other three came crashing through the ferns.

"*Shhhhhh!*"

"Sorry. Frank lost his boot in the mud and we had to find it," said Cass.

"I piggybacked him over the creek," said Danielle, who was still in her pajamas, saturated.

"Are the parents coming?" I asked.

"Didn't *you* tell them? We thought you did."

"Oh, *great!*"

No one would run back.

The climb up the side of the gully was a horror story, mainly for Frank. I'll just say we all made it to the gravel track, but Frank had more scratches than an old school desk. We crawled up and peered along the track. A hundred yards down to our left was the bulldozer, on the back of a truck.

"A low loader," whispered Zev.

"I hear music!" said Danielle.

"I can't see anybody," said Cass.

We started to crawl, but it killed our knees, so we took a chance and dashed across the track. Quickly we padded down to the bulldozer. There was no one there. The music was coming from somewhere farther on.

"Barry Manilow," whispered Danielle. "Blahh!"

We prowled around the truck. Zev swung up into the bulldozer cab and fiddled with something. Then someone laughed loudly. Mattock! We froze.

"Hide behind those bushes and watch the truck," I whispered to the others.

Danielle was about to protest, but I gave her my laser glare. Zev and I crept through the bush to find the source of the laugh.

God,
<u>Thank you</u> for Barry Manilow!

In a patch of sun, out of the breeze, Mad Mattock lounged in the open driver's-side door of a pickup, smoking. Auto, Mattock's son, and another tall skinny bloke, whose nose wasn't quite in the middle, sat casually on bags at the edge of the track. It was easier to hear Mad Mattock's booming voice. The other chap mostly just laughed. Auto hardly said a thing. I was so glad they didn't have a dog.

We wriggled as close we dared and lay behind a couple of trees. We could hear some of what they said.

"They're waiting for us to leave camp!" Zev whispered.

". . . and the messmates, while we're at it . . . the big one will make it all worthwhile . . . fiddleback . . . a new four-wheel drive . . . gonna have a dining table and chairs made from it . . . sell the rest to Melbourne . . . frothing at the mouth he was so bloody keen . . . greenies . . . like their fine bloody furniture, but they want their precious bush . . ."

Mattock was so smug, leaning there, smoking his cigarette. Auto nodded along and made pathetic echoes of what his father said.

Once those trees are gone, they are *gone*. Forever, I thought. The gully could give you a job, you fool. People would love to hike to this place and sit quietly and imagine the spirits and hear the stories about it. And then they would want to care more for other wild places. Couldn't these blokes "feel" the place? Were there so many gullies like it that this one could be wasted?

Barry Manilow stopped. Mattock flipped up a leather cover over his watch, checked the time, then took a pair of binoculars and looked through a gap in the bush.

". . . take 'em hours . . . all that junk back in . . ."

Then Mattock got out of the truck and did a mighty stretch. He was facing straight at us. I didn't dare look up, but we could hear every word.

"Jeez, I was lucky to get Thommo's dozer. He wants it up round Albury next week. It'd all be done if it wasn't for those

183

bloody city types. Feel like puttin' the dozer through the lot of 'em . . . know-all pregnant city cow . . . that kid, jeez, if she was mine, I'd teach her a thing or two. Did you hear about the snakes?" He laughed loudly. "Gave 'em something to think about."

Zev signaled to me furiously, then mouthed, "Come on! *Come on!*"

Under cover of Dolly Parton, we scraped, crawled, and scratched our way back to the others behind the truck.

"The tires!" I said.

Zev nodded.

The others were furious and arguing in whispers. "Took your *time*! Who's there? What's *happening*?"

We had to tell them everything to calm them down. "Shut *up*!" (It's hard to shout when you're whispering.) I know why TV dramas don't have five detectives charging around together!

"We're going to let the air out of the truck's tires."

"Cass! Keep watch on the bank. Wave if they come."

"Quick! Get a strong skinny stick and press the little valve in the middle like this . . . ," said Zev.

Hhssssssssssssssssssssssssssssssssssssssssssssssssssssss . . .

"Feel the air coming out? Just the tires this side, nearest the bank. *Hurry!*"

I got mine going. It seemed to take ages.

Hhsssssssssssssssssssssssssssssssssssssssssssss . . .

The tires were in pairs. Frank had an inside tire where the valve was near the ground. He crawled under, with the huge bulldozer on top of him. Danielle was lying half underneath, too. It was incredibly dangerous.

Hhssssssssssssssssssssssssssssssssssssssssssssssssss . . .

The truck slowly sank on one side. It was so scary. Where were the parents? I wished somebody, anybody—just one parent—would appear . . . please . . .

Hhsssssssssssssssssssssssssssssssssssssssss . . .

At that moment, the bed of the truck tipped and the ground at the edge of the track slipped as the dozer shifted. There was the sound of creaking metal as the chains holding the dozer on the truck bed strained.

Danielle rolled out and ran.

"Frank, GET OUT!" yelled Zev.

He scrambled away from the truck a split second before the restraining chain snapped like a rubber band.

Mattock and the other two raced around the corner just in time to see the massive weight of the bulldozer slowly slide half off the truck and rest its side on the bank.

Mattock stopped dead. "YOU ****ˆ%ˆ$%✲ %✲ ⊚⊚%$&ˆˆ✲ ˆ LITTLE &ˆ%$✲ ⊚ˆ&%&$&✲ ⊚✲ $Χ, MY GOD, I'LL ˆ&ˆˆ&ˆ%✲ ✲ ⊚%✲ &%ˆ+⌐✲ $% SKIN YOU %✲ ⊚✲ ˆ&ˆ%✲ ALIVE!"

We raced away down the track, hearts pounding.

"Spread out in the bush!" yelled Zev.

I slowed down for Frank and looked back.

"They're not after us! He's not following."

"What's happening?" said Cass.

"Are they getting the pickup?"

Zev stopped, then turned toward the truck again.

"Don't go back, Zev!"

"I think I saw him . . . get something . . ."

"No, Zev, he might have a *rifle!*"

Zev was pounding back to the truck.

"NO, ZEV!"

"Gone!" he yelled.

"What?"

"It's gone!"

"I thought he'd be so mad he'd kill us!"

"They can't use the dozer." Cass laughed.

"They've gone," said Frank.

"Good!"

"No, it's *not* good," said Zev, jumping down from the cab of the truck. "Mattock's taken his chain saw!"

"Oh no!"

I felt my heart flip over in my chest. How long could this go on?

"Which way'd they go?"

"Dunno, but I bet I know where they're going!" Zev was already running.

We slipped and slithered down into the gully like human pinballs. I saw Cass grab a branch in the nick of time at the top of a twelve-foot rock. Just as well we'd been leaping around the river like mountain goats.

Mattock was ahead of us, but he was carrying the chain saw, so he couldn't move fast. I had no idea what we'd do when we faced him. All I could think of was the chain saw. At the bottom of the track, we struck the boggy patch, like one of those nightmares where you're trying to run but you can't lift your feet.

They were at the fiddleback tree when we raced up.

"Please, you can't do this!" panted Cass.

"What can't I do?" growled Mattock, grappling with the chain saw. His left arm gave a violent yank. The engine spluttered and died. He ripped at the cord again. The chain saw screamed into life.

"I'll show you meddling little city twerps!" he roared above the chain saw. "I'll ringbark the damn thing in front of your bloody eyes."

"It's so *old*," I yelled. I felt hot and sick. I didn't think my legs would work.

"*No! Don't cut it!*" yelled Danielle.

He swung around and waved the chain saw at her.

"I'll cut *you*, you little witch!"

Zev flicked a stick at him, and suddenly the fight was on. Frank was throwing clumps, clods, sticks, anything. He darted in like a mosquito and kicked Auto in the ankle. My legs *did* work. I grabbed a dead fern frond and beat it at Auto, who defended his father as we attacked him from behind. Bent Nose had it in for Zev, and they chased and dodged furiously. Cass twanged a fern frond full in his face. It was frantic. Five kids against three fully grown men. I was terrified of what might happen.

But Mattock ignored us. He braced himself, feet apart, and set his thick shoulders. The saw bit into the blackwood, whining like a banshee, the noise rising higher and higher. Sawdust sprayed out.

Cass was screaming "Noooooooooo!" with tears flooding her eyes. She tripped as Bent Nose whacked her on the hip. In scrambled terror, we were screaming and screaming, *"Don't! Don't!"* Danielle was leaping around behind him, getting closer and closer, dodging Auto.

"Get away from him, Danielle! *Get away!*"

Then, from behind the enormous trunk, a weird figure suddenly appeared. "Dulugar!" screamed Frank.

Heap!

In that second, like a monkey, Danielle sprang onto Mattock's back.

"You little vermin!" he roared.

He tried to shake her off, still holding the chain saw. But no matter how he struggled, through the whole violent piggyback, Danielle clung on. She actually hit him twice!

"Get her *off me!*"

Auto grabbed Danielle by the arm and tried to wrench her away. The tip of the chain saw hit the tree and bucked back. As Danielle let go, Mattock lost his balance and stumbled toward Auto. In the scuffle, the saw screamed as it bounced up from Auto's boot.

Auto fell to the ground, writhing in agony.

Mattock dropped the saw.

The sound cut out.

There was a moment of silence, then Mattock grabbed Danielle by the upper arms and threw her, as if she was a doll. I saw her fly through the air! Like a crash-test dummy!

And this is the bit that makes me cry every time I remember it. Heap, who had run around behind them, flung himself to catch her as if he was diving after a football. Heap, who Danielle always dumped on and slagged off about, copped Danielle full in the chest. He slammed back, whacking his head on the trunk of a tree. He cushioned her fall.

Everyone froze as if we'd been stung. Heap lay there. I mean Clay, of course. Poor old Clay.

In the sudden quiet, we could hear shouting—the parents coming up the gully.

"Hey, what's *going on*?" It was Dad.

"Get up!" Mattock said to his son. For a second, Mattock put his hands on his hips as if he was going to take on everybody. Auto groaned in agony. Blood dripped from his boot as Bent Nose helped him stand.

"Make yourself scarce," snapped Mattock.

"What's *happening*?" Rob shouted. They were near.

Mattock picked up the chain saw to follow the other two. With a last scowl at us, he pushed through the ferns and was gone.

Sue brushed Heap's hair from his face. "He's breathing! Help me get him on his side."

Clay's eyelids flickered.

"Leave me alone! Leave me alone! The train . . ."

"He's back in the city," said Sue.

His face flicked through several expressions as his mind struggled to find itself.

"You're all right. Take it quietly," soothed Mum.

He blinked up at a crowd of faces. The only one missing was the one he'd come to find. He closed his eyes as if he'd given up. Then he opened them again and, breathing heavily, pushed himself into a sitting position.

"Come back to camp and rest," said Sue quietly, "then we'll take you into town and have you checked by a doctor."

Clay wobbled to his feet and, with Tibor's help, walked a few steps to the fallen log and flopped down on it, rubbing his head.

"You're in no fit condition . . . "

Clay waved him away. "I'm not an animal at the zoo. You don't have to feed me and take me to the vet." He looked at us as if we were children. Even though he was so hurt, he was strong.

Danielle stood still and quiet, out of the way, near Mr. Nic.

Then Heap, swaying like a drunk, got to his feet and set off to walk out of the gully.

"Thanks, Heap . . . s, Clay!" Danielle called after him.

He stopped. With an effort, he looked around. "That's okay."

"Go with him, Rob," said Sue.

Heap waved him away. "I know where I'm going."

"I went with him to a track," said Rob, "then he sat down and said he wouldn't move until I'd gone away. I stayed for an hour. What could I do? I couldn't carry him. I couldn't argue with him." Rob looked uneasy. "I left him there."

32
"Have You Got Five Minutes?"

We were packing up. Everybody was in a foul mood. It wasn't how it should have been at all. The parents were furious with us because we'd gone off without telling them, and because of the danger of the fight in the gully. Cass had a bruise like a purple saucer on her hip. There was still a lot of packing up to do, Donna was tired, the baby had been crying, we were late and wouldn't be home until well after dark, the tree was still in danger, and everyone was worried about Clay.

Then into Bacon Flat, carrying a sack, strolled Old Jim!

Timber bounded up to us, as if we were lifelong friends, and sniffed hello to Briquette.

"Have you got five minutes?" Old Jim was patting his pockets for his pipe. He caught Zev's eye, and he winked.

"Sure," said Dad. (He'd just shouted, "Come on, we should have left two hours ago.") "How about one last cup of tea?"

Old Jim settled himself in the chair Rob offered. "That'd be very nice."

Donna came around the car carrying the little boy.

"Well now, who's this new person?" said Old Jim.

"He was born here two days ago," said Donna proudly.

Old Jim studied the baby's chubby face. "He looks all right, doesn't he?" And he smiled his walnuttiest smile up into Donna's face.

"Actually, I must confess I knew about the arrival of this young man. A friend of yours has been helpin' me these last few days."

Old Jim found his pipe and put it in his mouth. "Now, down to business. I've got a few things to tell y' before y' go."

He tapped the pipe on the leg of the chair. "I always knew about that gully. Always wanted to own it and Bacon Flat, but Old Rushton didn't want to sell. Now, I was in no hurry. I've been waitin' a long time. What difference is a bit more time gonna make? I thought."

He took out his tobacco from the possum-skin vest.

"I had a little money in the bank. And found a bit o' gold from time to time." He laughed and scratched his head. "Had to find it all over again the other day! Had it hidden all round m' hut."

He filled the pipe with tobacco. "Finally, Old Rushton went off down to Bairnsdale hospital and died. His daughter in

Queensland wanted to sell this place to me, but I kept puttin' it off an' puttin' it off. Didn't want to go to town an' do all that paperwork business. Just never got around to it."

He patted his pockets for the matches. "But it's done now. This place belongs to me. Incidentally, you got a few phone calls to Queensland on y' phone bill. Very handy, those little phones."

He struck a match and lit his pipe. "Now, y' probably know more about what's growin' in that gully than I do, but I reckon there'd be things in there that'd be gone for good if the gully goes."

He took a long puff on his pipe. "It's mine now, and it's safe while I'm around. And when I've finished with it, when these hills have finished with me—" he looked at Donna "—it's yours. You can do what you like with it. But I don't want any tourists crawlin' around here till after I'm gone. And y' can bury me near that rock with the two trees close together, but don't go puttin' any headstone or anythin' like that."

"Thank you," said Donna simply.

"Does this mean the gully is *safe?*" I asked in amazement.

"What about Stan Mattock?" said Rob.

We waited through another long puff at the pipe. "Well now, one of the phone calls I made on that nice little phone of yours was to the lady who owns the timber mill. And I told her a thing or two." Puff, puff. "So I don't think we'll be havin' any trouble from him from now on."

Another reflective puff on the pipe. "Anyway, there'll be two of us on the lookout. He's got a bit of a headache at the moment, but that lad wants to stay 'ere. I'm gettin' a bit old, an' he likes the bush. Like me, doesn't mind it a bit rough. We're goin' to fit out the chicken shed for 'im. Might get another little Jersey cow."

He was an old man, and he'd thought it all out, and it was what he wanted. Old Jim felt very pleased with himself. He sat there like a farmer who's harvested the hay and got it all neatly in the shed.

I thought how absolutely amazing it was that, after all Donna's failed plans for him, in a funny way she *had* found a place where Heap—Clay—could fit in.

We were stunned by Old Jim's news, and for a while, we were unusually quiet. Even Danielle. It was a shock. Like winning the lottery. But then there were all the usual things that had to be said: what a wonderful vacation we'd had, and how everything had worked out in the end, and what a storm, and what a wonderful place it was, and fancy knowing Mr. Nic by parcel, and what a bonny baby, and thanks for the tea, and here are the newspapers and look after yourself, and tell Clay to get better, and thank you for everything . . .

"Well, you'd better get a move on, then," said Old Jim. "Y'

got a long way to travel. Sooner you than me. It's been very nice meetin' you all."

Everyone shook hands and gave Timber one last pat. Briquette and Timber had a last sniff of each other.

Then Old Jim picked up his sack, and with a nod and a wave, he headed off.

We scrambled around furiously, doing the last of the packing, trying to make up for lost time, but talking and laughing like mad things.

Then we heard a cough to get our attention. It was Old Jim back again.

"Nearly forgot—see, that's what happens when y' get old, y' forget what y' doin.' I got somethin' for you, miss," he said to me. "I won't be needin' it where I'll be going. Strikes me you care a lot about these things."

And out of the sack he took the fiddleback box and gave it to me.

"Be seein' ya."

33
Heading Home

Where the tents had stood, the yellow grass looked as if it had
been ironed. We'd worn paths around Bacon Flat, and we had
to cut the rope overhanging the river because the knot was so
tight. We picked up every atom of rubbish. We went for our
last swim and collected the plastic bag of things from Clay's
Talk Rock.

In the unsettling chaos of the packing, we saw Briquette trot
back to the pool where her hoof lay, just in case it had magically
surfaced.

"See, she *has* got a memory," said Frank.

It felt strange, climbing back into the cars. The Stella Street
tribe was dividing up into families again.

"Hop up! Hop *up*!" Briquette refused to jump into the car
and had to be lifted.

Donna sat across the backseat with the baby, packed around
with pillows. Danielle, Cass, and Frank went with Sue and

Tibor. Zev came with us. The ford had changed in the flood, but Sue and Tibor walked through it with sticks and found a route.

Going through the town, we stopped at the store for Dad to buy a new two-day-old newspaper to read while Mum was driving. I wanted a packet of Jaffas to help my return to the real world. The lady in the shop greeted us, all atwitter. She knew about the new baby and the boy with the wild hair.

"Ron!" she called out the back of the shop. "Ron! Come out here *quick*!"

Her dumpy husband appeared. "These are the people from Bacon Flat!" she said as if she was introducing royalty.

"Well, some of us from Bacon Flat," said Dad.

She refused to let Dad pay.*

Then she straightened up as if to say something that must be said properly.

"There are some good people in this town, and there are some good people at the mill, but, by golly, it's been hard these last few years. Right now there's a police car down at the mill," she said. "That's worth more to us than gold."

* When Danielle heard about this she said "you should have bought more!"

34
How Was Your Vacation?

James Blackwood O'Sullivan (Little Jim) is now three months old, and Donna's garden is going native. The Stella Street tribe tries to meet there on Sunday mornings for a long breakfast and a catch-up.

May and Maggs were extremely cheesed off when they heard what they'd missed out on. They say we are never to go on a vacation together again without them.

Donna had a phone call from Old Jim. (He's got a cell phone now, although he's only used it three times.) He rang to say Clay is good at milking, and the university people who are camped at Bacon Flat, studying the gully, have found a new sort of lizard.

Cass finished the knitting. Sue showed her how to cast off, which brought it to a stop. Then somehow Cass stuffed it and sewed it into a ball. So now it's back to a ball of wool again! It looks good—very bright—and Little Jim likes hitting it.

Remember how at the beginning I loved my new blazer? Well, I don't anymore. It's heavy, hot, and a bother because it cost so much and I have to look after it. Junior high school's good, though.

Donna keeps gum nuts in the little chest of drawers that Tibor made. She writes the name of the tree the nuts came from on the back of each drawer.

The treasures. Zev put in a last treasure that I'm not too sure about: a bulldozer fuse.

It was difficult to decide what to do with our treasures because different people found them, the mouse head belonged to all of us, and we felt they should stay together as souvenirs of our time on the river.

This is what we decided: the treasures would live in the fiddleback box, and I (ever-responsible Henni) would be the Keeper of the Treasures. If anybody wants their treasure, they can have it at any time. Frank, Danielle, and Cass took theirs to school for show-and-tell.

Donna gave us the Heart of the Pool to keep in the collection for Little Jim.

"After all," she said, "he's one of the gang."

As usual each morning, Dad reads the newspapers with every bit of bad news in the world boiled down and given scary headlines.

"Why aren't the good things ever news?" I asked.

FIVE KIDS HAVE ACE TIME SKINNY-DIPPING IN RIVER.

PREGNANT WOMAN DISCOVERS HEAVEN ON EARTH.

LITTLE AUSSIE BATTLER GIVES BIRTH BETWEEN TWO COOLERS.

FIDDLEBACK GULLY SAFE.

"What are you smiling at?" said Dad, who hadn't been listening.

MOTHER, BABY, AND PLAY CENTER DOING WELL.

When people ask me, "Did you have a nice time camping?" I just say, "Lovely, thanks," because if I tell them what really happened, they think I'm making it up, and it all takes so long to tell, and besides, I get embarrassed explaining what a placenta is.

But what a time we had.

Dear God,
I've thought a lot about how we got used to feeding Clay. It became normal but it was really un-normal.
We got so good at sneaking food we could be a shoplifting gang.
And we thought Clay was hopeless and we didn't think he could change, but he surprised us.
You have to watch what you get used to.

And another thing — well, two actually.
I own a beautiful fiddleback box,
which is rare wood, and I want to write
books, which is paper, and yet I'm
saying "Don't chop down trees."
Well... the box already existed
and I'll make the books worth the
paper they're printed on.

Do you think that's OK?
Henni

I really wanted Danielle's hiding place as an interesting finishing-off thing (I bet you're curious, too), so I waited till she was in a really good mood, then asked her.

"Diddle diddle fiddleback, you can't trick me."

She grinned and flung herself into a handstand. "You're not getting it out of me that way. Besides, it's not there anymore!"

Donna won't tell because it's Danielle's secret.

I guess we'll just
have to keep guessing!

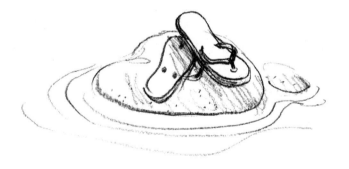

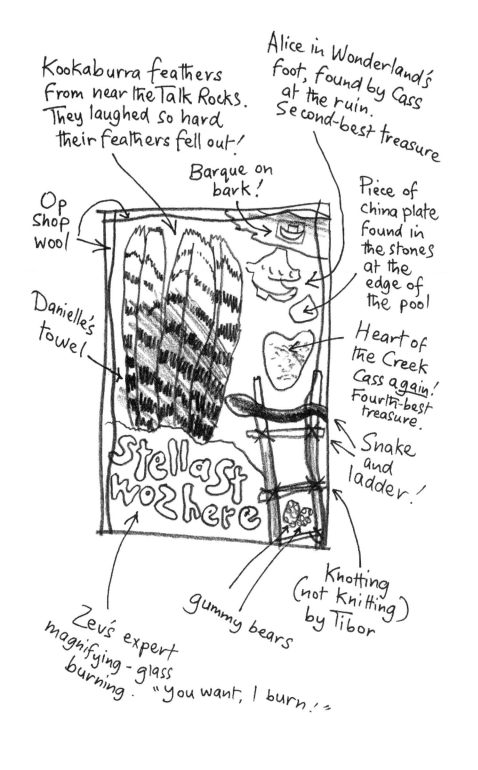

← Back cover

ABOUT THE AUTHOR

Elizabeth Honey is one of Australia's most popular authors. She began her career as an illustrator but has now published award-winning fiction, picture books, and poetry. Her novel *Don't Pat the Wombat!* was a Children's Book Council of Australia Honor Book in 1997.

Ms. Honey lives with her husband and two children in Melbourne, Australia.

CLEVE J. FREDRICKSEN LIBRARY
100 North 19th Street
Camp Hill PA 17011

DO NOT REMOVE
THIS CARD
$ FINE

CLEVE J. FREDRICKSEN LIBRARY
100 North 19th Street
Camp Hill, PA 17011

SEP   2001